The Frangipani Gardens

Barbara Hanrahan was born and grew up in Adelaide and is a leading printmaker as well as novelist. In the early 1960s she went to London to study at the Central School of Art, and since then has taught in art schools both in England and Australia. She has had many one-woman exhibitions and her work appears in the Australian National Gallery and most state galleries. Her first book, *The Scent of Eucalyptus*, was published in 1973. Hanrahan is now the author of seven novels, including *Where the Queens all Strayed* (UQP, 1978), *The Peach Groves* (UQP, 1979), and *Dove* (UQP, 1982). She now lives in Adelaide.

By the same author —

The Scent of Eucalyptus
Sea-Green
The Albatross Muff
Where the Queens all Strayed
The Peach Groves
Dove
Kewpie Doll

Barbara Hanrahan

The
Frangipani
Gardens

University of Queensland Press

ST LUCIA ● LONDON ● NEW YORK

First published 1980 by University of Queensland Press
Box 42, St Lucia, Queensland, Australia
Reprinted 1984

Printed in Australia by Dominion Press—Hedges & Bell

Distributed in the USA and Canada by the University of Queensland Press,
5 South Union Street, Lawrence, Mass. 01843 USA

Cataloguing in Publication Data

National Library of Australia

Hanrahan, Barbara.
  The frangipani gardens.

  I. Title. (Series)

A823'.3

Library of Congress

Hanrahan, Barbara.
  The frangipani gardens.

  I. Title.
  PR9619.3.H3F7   1984   823   84-19670

ISBN 0 7022 1563 5

To Reece Nobes

Wilt thou go with me sweet maid
Say maiden wilt thou go with me
Through the valley depths of shade
Of night and dark obscurity
Where the path hath lost its way
Where the sun forgets the day
Where there's nor life nor light to see
Sweet maiden wilt thou go with me

John Clare

Part One

Boy and Girlie

And Granma said "You are the descendant of an Irish race of kings." You must remember it when you didn't fancy the white of your egg, when it was Betsy Brown pudding for tea; when Mama looked worse and it was your fault: wasting disease they called it and, at the last, foam came out of her mouth, the doctor looked weary as he wiped it away. And Papa was a wild man, crying; he was only a child, younger than you — throwing himself on the bed, grasping her cold hand. But he hated you. It was you who did it — killed her. You were too big as a baby, Boy O'Brien. Coming out, you tore her; you rent her private places.

They took her away and Papa didn't talk to you. Papa worked in the shop, selling the little packets of seeds. Nothing was better than looking at those packets — you had a secret garden all your own. You shuffled them; held them to your ear and rattled. Who'd imagine that those bullet-hard seeds could sprout stems and petals and sticky pollen dots.

A lady came twice a week to do artistic floral arrange-

3

ment. Leaves fell like green rain over the floor, and the stems of hydrangeas were scraped, roses were banged, dahlias scalded. This lady did magic — scraping and banging, slitting and pricking. Almond blossom lasted if you immersed it in sugar water; beech branches were preserved in glycerine. Some flowers had wire stems . . . for a dead baby you could have a pillow of freesias. Mama had a snowdrop cross.

And God was Love, but St Stephen was the first martyr — they dragged him outside the city; angrily, they aimed their rocks. And St Peter died upside down; St Lawrence frizzled on the gridiron. Granma opened her book and horrors emerged, they waited to get you at night. But your ancestor was Brian Boru; there were three lions on your crest; "The strong hand uppermost" was your motto.

Girlie was always the favourite. She was ugly, a dwarf, they ought to sell her to the circus. She'd been a baby who lived in cotton-wool, and had slipped from Mama's body so easy. One minute Mama sat down to drink a cup of tea, next minute Girlie emerged. It was a story put in the newspaper: about Girlie's tiny perfection. She was one of the little people, a fairy baby given on a whim. At her birth Mama heard sweet music like melodeons and fifes. But it was only a story. Girlie was small, certainly, but she'd never do as a rival to the Cincinnati speck of humanity.

In the beginning they weren't Girlie and Boy. She was Kathleen, he was Pat; it was Adelaide, but they owned proper Irish names, bestowed with a holy water sprinkle. But Mama died and then Mass stopped — you weren't anything then.

Girlie always wheedled a cuddle. She was older than Boy, but she was treated as little sister. She was a draw-

4

ing room charmer, dimpled and lisping, but when she had you alone she'd pinch, and: Do this, she'd say, do that. Or she'd start off on her mocking silvery laugh, and the thing that meant most lost its flavour. What did he want with those seed packets? It was unnatural . . . constantly fiddling with them — a great boy like that.

He grew careful. Nothing should betray him again. He kept away from the florist's shop with its moist secret smells. Feeling made you vulnerable, so Boy gave it up. Courage, lad. As you strengthen the body, so will the mind become strong. Go in for games, take lots of exercise and a cold bath each morning. You will live to laugh at your fears yet.

He turned into a scholar, someone who lived through his mind. He had an athlete's body, he used the dumb bells daily, but he didn't see the strong brown limbs or the boxer's chest. A mind was the main thing, Boy's was wonderfully rational. The lovely finality of history — all those dates that heralded all those countless endings — was what he liked best. Dates and death and war — that was history for Boy. The true heir by blood. Direct and perpetual antagonists. Mortal wounds, treasonous intrigues . . . history was real.

But up the top of the house, sitting like a witch in a grotto, was Granma. Papa kept her hidden away. She had ringlets and rouged cheeks; she had two mouths, because her lipstick had slipped. And her chamber pot was always in view, though she stank of cachous as much as piddle, for she constantly sucked on something sweet. "Try one, Boy," she'd command, proffering a crumpled paper bag. And you were helpless, you couldn't refuse, but must crunch at sickly sweetness as she looked you over. Old half-wit — belching and farting in her basket chair, ruining Boy's neat rule of not feeling.

Granma was a back number who should have died years ago. Boy would have allowed her that first Mayoral Ball in the Town Hall in '66 that she reminisced of constantly (imagine, a crinolined Gran dancing the merry polka under crystal chandeliers), then wiped her out. She would have stayed Eily Casey then, and none of those O'Briens would have existed — Mama would never have died.

Though Granma had been an evil harbinger from the start. She thrived on blight and misfortune . . . Gran, back in those penniless County Cork days: carrying buckets of mulch suspended from a yoke across her infant shoulders, then going home to memorize miracles and the stations of the cross, and make a start on that legendary sampler in silks that proclaimed "Look at this, and you may see what care my parents took of me". Was it true? — little Eily plying her needle, a junior Penelope awaiting her royal husband, while outside the pigs scrimmaged and Dadda's arm had turned septic, he could not work: there was only cabbage for tea — really?

But the famine was true. The year 1847, and over sixty years later there was someone still alive to scare Boy with an eyewitness account.

And the spring of the previous year had been unpromising enough. Hail and sleet fell in March, and in Belfast there was snow as late as the first week in April. But when the summer came it made amends. The weather in June was of tropical heat; vegetation sprang up with rapidity and a splendid harvest was anticipated. But at the end of the month the weather broke; there were copious downfalls of rain, the air was electrical and disturbed. There was much lightning, accompanied by thunder, and after that intense cold. Yet still the potato

6

crop flourished; all over the country were fields of waving green. Then, in the early days of August, a strange portent was seen simultaneously in several parts of Ireland. A fog, which some described as white and others as yellow, was seen to rise from the ground. It was dry and emitted a disagreeable odour; it bore the blight within its accursed bosom. The work of destruction was swift. That night the fresh green potato leaves were mottled with dark spots such as would come from a drop of acid; by morning they were bleached and withered and stinking. Throughout the whole country the entire crop was destroyed, almost to the last potato.

And you didn't want to listen, but Granma made you. Her cracked voice held you — you were in the grip of death, back there with Eily. Wringing your hands and wailing bitterly, wandering the highroad, grasping at anything that promised sustenance.

Even if Boy stopped up his ears, even if he ran from the room, her voice could still find him. At night it soundlessly whispered, it made him see: the dry tongue, shrunk to half its size and brown in the centre; the thin bloodless lips, coated with sores . . . discoloured sodden skin, putrid smell, and Eily out there alone, dodging fever hospitals and coffin ships. And it didn't matter that the nuns saved her from the gutter, for now Eily had turned into Mama — and it was Boy who did it: fighting for life, he put her in the way of dying. And then St Lawrence was there, but changed from the gentle-faced man in the ray of light holding the palm branch. He wasn't saying that the sick and poor were the treasures of the Church, now. His skin peeled off in layers, he shrieked as the flames leapt higher. And Boy was asleep, but he was crying. For it was the fire Gran said would get them because Papa hadn't taught them religion. For he was feeling. He felt the flames. And the gallant Wolfe's mortal wound, the Black Hole growing stuffier, the pillow coming down on the Princes in the Tower. Feeling was awful. History was ruined.

School was a prison, but home was worse. This creature had come to work for Papa. She was a girl, she made you think of a snake. It was the way she stood — sinuous. Which meant characterized by or abounding in turns, curves . . . deviating from the right, morally crooked. Boy looked the word up in the dictionary and used it against her. "Sinuous," he muttered when he saw her. The word was a defence, a charm.

Pearl was a mystery, she was Church of Christ. Which meant you drank lemonade and didn't jig or wear lippy. But she had a habit of moistening her lips with her tongue — Pearl's tongue was shiny and pink; she was always smoothing her dress, settling her hips. She was skinny, sway-backed; but she had this little stick-out stomach. She flaunted it at Boy. She was pale, neutral-tinted, with a thin rat mouth, pointed teeth. She had these eyes, though — china-blue, shadowy underneath. Her eyes were dreamy in her dry pale face. They pretended not to see you; Pearl's eyes skitted away when she talked. But she was always watching through the window when Boy came home from school.

Pearl served behind the counter, she arranged the shop window, her fingers did wonders with wire and twine, scissors and tape as she bound and probed and cut. She made wedding bouquets and buttonholes, shoulder sprays and posies, and you never guessed at the false stalks, the cunning stitches, the cruel silver wires that snaked through those stems. She was a dab at flowers for condolence, last tributes of affection and esteem. Gates of heaven, harps, flags and cushions were superbly worked in mass blooms.

As a bonus she got on with Gran. Oddly, the old girl liked her. They jabbered together about their different Jesuses, sometimes Pearl sang — hymns that sounded like love songs. Despite most of their words being gloomy, she crooned them happily enough. Blood was outpouring, the glorious western sun was sinking, shades were deepening, the path was thorny, but Pearl was marching, marching, ever onward marching where the saints had trod.

Then one day she asked Boy to help her fetch vases from the storeroom. Her eyes entreated him, and the door closed behind them, and somehow she had him. Boy was on the floor with the bag of silver sand and the watering can with the bent spout. He would never forget. Her slippery Italian-cloth apron, the greasy smell of her hair. He despised her, but those were his hands on her body — feeling, finding: the liver-coloured birthmark, the crimped pattern of knicker elastic, the tiny breasts under her singlet. She had her eyes shut, her mouth hung open as if to shout *Alleluia*. Her mouth was a wet snail, her tongue felt slimy, like the stems of decaying flowers. Pearl — who marched onward, who fain would mount and penetrate the skies — had turned into an upside-down beetle, scrambling, waving her legs. Boy lay above her and stopped being excited. For he would crush her, kill her as dead as Mama. Oh God. And then he was strong, he fought her, slid off her, and knew: Never again.

Pearl hated him after that. Inside her mouth her tongue hissed poison, her teeth wanted to tear him apart. Her eyes saw through Boy, now, as her fingers did what someone else's had done long ago — scalded the stems of dahlias, burned the ends of poppies, stripped the rose of all its thorns.

Then everything changed. The shop was sold, for Papa had bought an estate at Fern Gully, in the Adelaide Hills, that would do for a model nursery. The Frangipani Gardens would specialize in exotics.

And Pearl got married. She chose a Pommy with skin the colour of milk. Jim Reed had sandy hair and eye-lashes so pale you hardly saw them.

He was one of the fellows who worked in Papa's garden. Boy dodged him, for Pearl would have told about that time in the storeroom. Yet had she? — perhaps not, for Jim smiled at Boy and they started talking, and it seemed that they were friends. But how could Jim bear it with Pearl? Boy couldn't understand. Not even when Jim confided that it was hard in a strange country, and a new chum had to seize his chances.

For a while Pearl's songs brightened up. It was "Hail, happy day! . . . " and "Jerusalem the golden . . . " as she pushed Gran about in a Bath-chair, to drink in the tonic Hills air.

Jim stopped feeling the wedded bliss first. Boy and he began taking long walks away from the nursery.

Boy had never been happier. He went to a Catholic school, now; he felt as if he belonged. And it was cheering to have a friend, to be men together. With Jim he felt another person. Indeed, Jim couldn't abide the "Boy"; to Jim, he was Pat.

But at school his grades got lower; he was the oldest in his class. Instead of working, he dreamed . . . of the way Jim's eyes wrinkled to mere slits when he smiled, of the sandy hairs on his arm. Of that other life he'd lived across the sea, in a world Boy couldn't imagine. Sometimes a pinched look came on Jim's face when he reminisced. He was back home again, he hadn't escaped after all. Sometimes, then, he'd gather a few flowers for

10

Pearl. Good old wifey; her tongue was sharp, but she'd saved quite a nest egg.

And then in Sarajevo the Archduke died, and men started marching away. All that year Pearl watched Boy and Jim with narrow eyes — her eyes had a cunning look as she and Granma cackled together.

Jim Reed began talking about the Tommies, the Aussies, the Froggies, the Belgies, the Pork and Cheese.

One day he told Boy he was going. Over there. Britain's foes must learn that Britain's sons were men of bulldog breed.

Boy sailed, too. He was old enough — just, to be as much a soldier as Jim. No one could stop him donning khaki: no one tried. On Boy's last day at school, instead of being written off as a dullard, he was celebrated as a hero. The headmaster shook his hand and bade a speedy and safe return.

You felt strange at Suez when you saw the troop-ship *Ballarat* leave for Australia with the first batch of wounded from Gallipoli. But a thrill passed through you at the sight of the ancient monuments. And the mode of tilling the earth was the same as in the days of Christ.

Boy was happy, even though Reveille was at four o'clock daily. For being with Jim was so natural. There was nothing soppy, they didn't talk much. Only once, Jim spoke of after the war. How they'd go back to the Hills — but deeper in, far from Fern Gully; how they'd have some land of their own. Boy would grow flowers, maybe they'd have a cow.

Then it was March, and training was over. They reached Marseilles and somewhere north was a battle line, but they didn't think of it yet. The train pulled out of the station, and it was La Belle France, with the trees clothing themselves in new season's raiment and the hedges sparkling with dew.

11

The landscape changed as they drew further north, and on the third night of their journey they ran into a severe snowstorm. They had left the genial south behind and found, instead, a country where winter held sway.

War meant mostly mud and carrying rations in the dark along duckboards. Nightly, Boy made the pilgrimage along Wine Avenue and Paradise Alley. The guns were always at it, the aeroplanes went over like hawks. Boy thought a lot about noises. How shells shrieked, and machine gun bullets spat. But thinking could get on your nerves. The trenches were uncanny, it was a queer old war. But it was honour and glory. Remember: One day mud will fly, and we shall be after the Kaiser's pet dog in Berlin — if he has escaped the sausage machine.

It was Hell, of course, but they came out of it. Now they were marching towards the push on the Somme, and for a while they halted beside fine growing crops of wheat. And Boy and Jim went across the big field that was a patriotic blaze of poppies and daisies and corn-flowers, and sat on the bank of a stream. They were away from the war; they were covered by a bush. Boy and Jim didn't want a house with walls that might come tumbling down — no, for them there was the bush with its wallpaper of green and these little creamy blossoms, and past that sky-blue. And Boy wanted to talk about big things, he started to, but Jim joked the terrible emptiness — all the lost dead ever-after time that would come later — away, and they fell to playing like school-boys, to rest themselves from the war. They jumped and took turns at leapfrog and Boy tore his shirt trying to throw Jim at wrestling. By dinnertime they were tired, but then the order came to fall in. They sang as they marched through the village. They sang "Goodbyee, don't cryee, don't sighee, wipe the tear, baby dear, from your eyee". That was the favourite song.

Then the landscape was a huge quagmire. For all the world it looked as if some gigantic plough had churned things upside down. And you had cramp and trench-foot and your boots got sucked away by the mud; and then it was that Sunday — you were advancing. Is that what it was, did you guess what you were doing? — when you came to the slope and it was daylight, and the enemy gunners and snipers used their weapons with deadly effect. Yes, the sniping qualities of the enemy proved fearful, but Boy gripped his rifle and ran through the hail — it was easy, like dodging the drops of a shower. And he lay in a shell-hole and now it was night, and a great fire was burning low through the misty darkness. It was a nightmare, with the wounded groaning round him and Boy had seen it happen — the large gap cut in the lines of our advancing troops, as the military report would tell it. And Jim was among them: Jim fell, he died. And Boy was alone, alive, and he didn't care anything about Liberty or Honour of the Homeland. He forgot even Jim, he only remembered Granma and the terrible Irish tales . . . All over the country iron boilers were set up in which Indian meal stirabout was boiled, and round them on the roadside there daily moaned and shrieked and fought and scuffled crowds of gaunt cadaverous creatures.

Boy didn't care, as all round him the dying moaned, but he did it for Jim — perhaps. It was written up, he got the medal. "Among the courageous and unselfish deeds for which decorations were awarded, the most admired throughout the Battalion was that of Private P. O'Brien, D.C.M. Rapidly gaining the enemy's first trench, he made his way single-handed to the ultimate

objective, accounting for fourteen of the enemy..."
They called it peaceful penetration. He did it with rifle
and bayonet and Mills' bomb, with the inner armour of
self-initiative and confidence. It was described as sheer
audacity. And then he fell down, and all round him were
shadows and spectres, the impersonations of disease
and famine, stalking to the general doom.

As soon as she saw him she knew they were strangers.
Though she smiled with all the others and ran forward
to bury her face in his tunic. Flags waved and there was
bunting and a big WELCOME HOME across the street.
Boy wore khaki and his medal and cameras clicked, re-
porters scribbled in their pads. Boy's mouth opened and
shut, it mentioned pluck and gallant comrades. Gents
blew their noses and ladies cried when it came to the
poetic bit about battlefields covered with poppies, and a
tiny lark rising. It was pathetic, Girlie wanted to hear of
skulls sprouting from the mud like mushrooms and
Prince Charles of Prussia's azure aeroplane. Boy was a
Sunday School hero with a sickly grin, shaking even
Papa's hand as if he loved him.

Once Papa had been only Girlie's; once he'd been a
man, fierce and beautiful. He'd paid Boy back with cold
indifference for pushing Mama towards her grave. But,
when Boy was away at the war, Papa's heart let him
down. Overnight, the terrible autocrat was replaced by a
weak-hearted puppet; his tyrant's face was betrayed by
an idiot grin. From being as good as the pantomime
devil he'd turned into a comic Mr Punch. The pity hurt
Girlie like a knife: she hated Papa for causing such pain,
as much as she hated Boy. It was the war that had done

it, people said — sometimes Girlie even believed it. Blaming the war made it Boy's fault, meant he'd killed Papa as surely as Mama.

But Girlie was clever, she kept her thoughts to herself. Even Granma and Pearl never guessed how badly she felt. Though Pearl got close sometimes, for Pearl was a dab at hating, too.

Jim had died. Boy O'Brien had dragged him off to the war and plunged Pearl into mourning for life. The gloom cast by the death of a dear one generally left you without heart for forms and ceremonies — Pearl was an exception. She didn't wish to be spared any share in the mournful details. Dead, Jim belonged to her as he never had alive. Each year she remembered him with a poem in the newspaper:

> Just when life was brightest,
> Just when his hopes were best,
> His country called, he answered,
> Now in God's hands he rests.

Pearl was a mourner *par excellence*, a natural for the livery of woe. After Jim died all her dresses were suitably sombre; she bestrung herself with jet beads. A hairnet worn low on the brow was a symbolic widow's cap; her black silk petticoat and stockings showed grief had penetrated to her innermost sanctuaries.

Her room was funereal, too, with its permanently lowered blind. On one side of the vase of woolwork pansies was a portrait of Jim in uniform; on the other, Jim again, in civvies.

Pearl was a riddle. She sang that she was the white flower of a blameless life, but her tongue liked to linger on smut. Her hush-hush voice was a generous voyeur, always willing to share the peep-show.

15

She was only paid help, but Girlie couldn't keep away. Right from the start, from her florist shop days, Pearl was the person Girlie liked most. It was ridiculous, thank goodness no one guessed, but Girlie and Pearl were alike. They were both perfectly evil, perfectly strong — it seemed that way to Girlie . . . though, of course, she was only pretending. Imagining was a habit; Girlie had started early on. It was an antidote to her miniature size, and the attendant sweetness everyone expected.

After listening to Pearl, life seemed merely a matter of bodies touching. Yet, as you urged on your Gully escort of the evening, your mind kept cool. It meant nothing at all, no sin was involved. It was utterly disappointing, but for ages afterwards Girlie felt defiled.

Then it was an afternoon when she sat in Pearl's twilight room. Outside, the sun was shining — it was hot, quite Indian summer, and all through the Hills the nagging rattle of seed-pods sounded. And as Pearl talked she watched Girlie slyly, it was almost as if she were playing. Then Pearl edged closer on the sofa: her silk petticoat made a *frou-frou*, it rustled invitingly and Girlie weakened. She couldn't bear it, her body would send her mad; there was a feeling deep inside her, as if a giant finger made forcible ingress. And then Girlie knew no shame, she pressed herself against Pearl's mournful bodice. For once, it seemed something interesting might happen, but Pearl hesitated (it was only for an instant), and Girlie's mind got clear. She saw what she was doing, and the fever in her body let her down. Girlie's nose wrinkled. Cool-headed, her ardour abated, Pearl's body smelled decidedly sour.

After that, Girlie recognized the danger of her near defeat. It was humbling to fall so easily into another's power. Pearl was strong, therefore Girlie must be stronger; she must know more.

For instance, there was a lady who lived off Wakefield Street, Adelaide, near the Christian Brothers' College. Well, Mrs Karioli, like Pearl, always wore black — which was fitting, for you visited her to make contact with a departed loved one. Mrs K. was a medium and, because of the war, business was looking up.

Girlie started learning of visions and voices, levitation and speaking with tongues. She went to seances where spirits announced their identity with the aid of a roll-call from the alphabet, and there were luminous hands and accordion music played at a distance. It was wonderful, wasn't it — how Mama sent her message telling that she longed to hold you in her arms? Yes, Girlie was as bewitched as all the others; she clutched her heart, she sobbed as bad. But even as she did, her mind stayed cold, her mouth wanted to giggle at the gullible ninnies — Girlie among them — who sat with little fingers touching, obediently believing in their tame spirit world.

For Girlie didn't want tameness, sameness, safety. Inside her miniature body was an ogre, longing to get out. Oh, why did she live now, in commonplace times — why couldn't she have existed when there were giants in the earth? Constantly, Girlie longed for other ages, when monsters of impiety were the norm.

It was the one she loved who'd stunted her most. Girlie had been maimed early on. The reward of Papa's tyrant arms about her had set her off playing little girl for life. Yet all the time: Damn, blast, devil take it! — while a docile Girlie sat on Papa's knee and breathed in his heady man-smell, a stranger Girlie jeered inside her head and spat out the silent maledictions that cut at the sentimental fug. After Mama went — after Boy was born and Girlie relied on Papa for love — it was always like that: Girlie was always two.

So it was easy to run forward with a welcoming smile when the boy-hero came home from the war. United, Boy and Girlie made a striking pair. No one would have guessed the extent of their enmity.

Yet there was a moment, early on, when their relationship stood a chance of being different; when Girlie was given an opportunity to change it to something warm and alive.

They were walking in the orchard by the creek when, without warning, Boy began to talk of Jim. It was as if he couldn't help himself; he wouldn't be silenced, and the awful thing was, that part of her understood. Girlie, who had loved Papa, wanted to hold Boy close and comfort him; wanted to push away the barrier of hating that had been there all the years. But the Girlie whose name was down in the Social Notes jumped back.

What would people say if they knew? Boy was a fool to let the mask drop. For you must always keep pretending. It was all right for Boy to love a man — quite the done thing, in fact, Queer Street being a fashion of the moment. But you did it lightly — with an ironic smile and lots of back-chat. You didn't say "I loved him" with tears in your eyes.

It was easy to silence him, she didn't have to waste many words. Just enough to let him know it was filthy. But amusing. But she didn't want to hear any more.

They disliked each other, yet they were brother and sister — in a curious way each needed the other, for each gave the other identity. He was Boy, she was Girlie: they were a pair, no questions asked. Year after year they kept up with all that was new. They were tops at politesse over teacups, their feet moved in strict tempo as they danced away nights with latest steps. They never made the mistake of expressing an opinion, you were never bothered to get to know them.

It was Girlie's fault that things went wrong.

Boy came back from the war one of the living dead. Apart from that shaming mention of Jim in the orchard, he gave no sign of feeling. If he went off now and then for a measure of dissipation, he did it discreetly — you were never embarrassed by a rumour. But Girlie was different, part of Girlie got bored. For that giant inside her kept living — it stayed a fidgety nuisance that couldn't be paid off with compliments, or flattered out of existence by the successes of a social whirl.

All the time she was so lonely. Though there was Papa to remind her of what she'd lost and Boy to hate and Granma to scorn and Pearl to . . . was it fear or love that Girlie felt for Pearl?

She took little comfort from her surroundings. Even as she paid lip service to Papa's nymphea pond, to the frangipanis which gave the estate its name, she dismissed them. They'd belonged to others first. The house and its grounds, the orchards and market-gardens about them, were constant reminders that Girlie O'Brien was small. Papa had brought them here on false pretences. It was someone else's stately home they lived in: Papa was a nobody who'd made money from selling seeds.

And when you strayed off the Gully Road, the hills encircled you; the gum trees humped together; the sky rose higher — you felt more and more alone. The real Gully country was gloomy and malevolent. The trunks of the gums were cold and polished as bone. It was an old old country. Who were you? Why were you there?

Then one day Mr Teakle from the jam factory came

19

to inspect Papa's exotics. Hazel, his daughter, accompanied him. She was an innocent — rabbit-mouthed, moony-eyed. Peaches and cream complexion, hair that made you think of a sheep. A good girl, Hazel, modest. She blushed when Girlie took her hand.

And walking side by side through Papa's greenhouses, they came to a perfect place. There were leaves like tea trays, and stems making monkey-ladders, and orchids frilled everywhere. Hazel Teakle. The orchids rose in tiers; they looped overhead to form a flaming jungle roof. Each morning Girlie spread Teakle fig on her toast.

She came to see Girlie every day. They talked; they sat silent. They were friends, it was a comfortable feeling. With Hazel, Girlie didn't mind being tiny; she no longer felt she must dance faster, dress smarter, talk harder than all the rest or else she might disappear.

Pearl was always watching them, her eyes were cold. Hazel shivered, but Girlie didn't care. She was a new person. The split that had divided her all those years had healed, and Girlie felt reborn.

But she wasn't strong enough to stay whole. The giant triumphed, a storm started raging in Girlie's head. She loved Hazel, but she scorned her, too. And it was the best excitement yet. Girlie felt herself grow larger than life. Soon Pearl would be no one to fear; through Hazel, Girlie would succeed where she'd failed.

Yet Girlie hadn't planned it. She hadn't meant to . . . Why did it happen?

Why did the voice keep saying it? "Do you love me?" the voice kept asking — a familiar voice, persistent. And it was Girlie's, of course, but it sounded like another's. The strange thing was, that, even as Girlie's mouth said the words, the voice sounded like Pearl's. It asked on and on. "Do you love me?" it pestered — whining, wheedling. And Hazel said she did, but it wasn't good enough. For if she did, why didn't she, wouldn't she? — why not agree, why was it wrong? The voice went on — cajoling, urging — and now Hazel was sobbing and Girlie knew she had won. Hazel's hands fluttered, then they were still. She was sighing, saying it was wrong. Then a dove started cooing in her throat.

So it was done, and the precious thing ruined. Girlie had triumphed terribly — she was more alone than ever. Hazel had been proved as worthless as everyone else. But the hypocrite still lisped her *I love you*s, even as Girlie told her it was a sin; that she didn't want to see her again. It was thrilling. It only took minutes, a few words, and Hazel was someone mad. She left the model nursery in a dream. Girlie began to giggle. Pearl came out on to the drive and stood beside her. Pearl was laughing, too, as they watched Hazel go away.

And now Girlie pretended a new thing. She said I am a witch. She said Yes, I am perfectly evil. And she took Pearl's advice and wrote to Melbourne for the set of books. They had a star made of triangles on the cover; they told secret wicked things.

For a while Hazel kept coming back. She stood at the gates of The Frangipani Gardens, twisting her hands. She looked awful, a fright. She was dying of love, the Gully said. People wondered who had caused it. Some said Boy, others whispered another name. They stopped talking when Girlie went by. But that was ages ago. People started to forget. To most of the Gully, it seemed, now, that Hazel had always been lacking.

Part Two

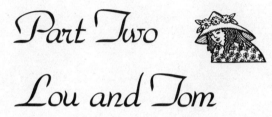

Lou and Tom

1

The town was really quite near, though the scrub and the sandhills disguised the fact. Lou was the princess who waited, as she stood on the verandah and swept. It was her task, she must sweep up every speck of sand. Swish-swish, went her broom — and if she did, if she swept the verandah quite clean, something wonderful would happen. There was the Prince of Wales, there was Rod La Rocque. But Valentino was dead, and the wind kept blowing. Every day there was more sand, and you had to go to town, there was always shopping to do.

In town people stared, ladies whispered behind their gloves. Tom was odd, with his staring eyes, and in summer he went brown as a blackfellow. The ladies whispered, they drew together. Why isn't he at school? . . . Yes, the image of her mother . . . But Ella wasn't ashamed of her body. She'd yawn and you saw the fluff in her armpit; her skin was soft, you saw the shape of a nipple. Compared to her, Lou was merely a lump, and it had happened — she bled every month, it was awful. A proper girl was pliant as a willow-wand;

the Berlei corset ad reckoned the theme to be slenderness. And there was the shingle, the Hindenburg crop, but Lou stayed a fat girl with hair like Rapunzel's.

Sometimes, when Tom was sleeping, she got out of bed and stood before the mirror and undid the plait. Her hair made a shawl, it was crinkly, all gold, though you couldn't see properly in the dark. She was blurred in the mirror and she let her nightie fall. She felt wicked: she was big and creamy like Ella — in the dark she almost believed it. And will go the same way, said the ladies in town. For their mother was bad, it was because of the men. Now and then they came through the scrub; they left their buggies on Parrot Road, the man with the black moustache had a car. They smiled at Lou and Tom as they went up the path, but when you saw them in town they didn't know you. When a man came, Lou and Tom went away from the house. Further from town, past the red gums that in winter stood in water. There were insects on the native peach trees — those trees were sickly. Apple berry crept up trunks; running postman was everywhere.

That plant was red; bridal creeper was white. Like the soursobs along the cliffs it was a common weed, its seeds spread by starlings and blackbirds. Lou liked to pick bits and put them in her hair. In the sun her plait looked on fire, all the small hairs that edged it were flames. A bride, she would be a bride in a Limerick lace veil. Lou mooned, dodging three-cornered Jacks, while Tom concentrated on the birds.

For they were out of the scrub, now, they were through the sedge swamps: they'd reached the lagoon. The water was fresh, not salt; sometimes it was covered with ducks.

Round the lagoon was a thicket of tea-tree. Tom and

Lou had a tunnel. They squeezed through (it was dark, the tunnel might have been dug in the earth), and once nests were everywhere; once the tea-tree was one moving mass of wild fowl of every description. Nests hung on every branch, containing eggs and young birds and old ones — myriads of them, known and unknown. The birds gazed at Lou and Tom; their tameness was marvellous.

They waded in water under which were fallen tea-tree twigs. It was hard to balance, for if you put out a hand to steady yourself, you might squash a fledgling. The noise of the birds was deafening; when Tom shouted their babble grew worse. There were all sorts of ducks — teal and whistlers and widgeons, and those ones with the rainbow necks. There was a big tree on which perched several eagle-hawks; under it was a bank of swan feathers and bones, for the hawks usually killed a swan each day.

In the beginning the lagoon belonged only to Lou and Tom and the birds, and the blackfellow whose name was King Billy. Lou had never seen him, but Tom had. Tom saw him standing at the end of the tunnel . . . and the ducks ran out like a stream of bullets from a machine gun — straight into Billy's net.

Probably, though, Tom made Billy up. He told whoppers sometimes, and would talk to crusader bugs and jewel beetles, for his own world was better than school. Ella didn't care when he said he wouldn't go. One day the Inspector came to the house. His boots sank into the sand, they trampled the noon-flowers by the gate. But their mother made it all right. She told of Tom's fits and how she dosed him with Trench's remedy. Her dress was low cut, she showed the tip of her tongue when she talked. Tom was saved. He went on reading in the

27

encyclopedia about the rufous fantail, the pallid cuckoo. Tom didn't talk much, but he was clever. He was only eight, but he seemed an old man.

But you didn't see so many birds, now. Not since the man started coming with his gun. It had a double barrel and when he fired a million birds rose; they shadowed the sun, they darkened the day. It was the man with the moustache who visited Ella: he smiled as he picked up dead ducks. But the Cape Barren geese still came to the lagoon in May, on their way to Lakes Alexandrina and Albert; at early morning the swamp was blue with bald coot. Though it wasn't so good any more. People took away the tea-tree for fencing and firewood; the man was always there.

His car was a Hudson Super Six. He had Zig-zag cigarette papers and sat with his legs apart. Shall I love him? thought Lou, lying awake in the dark. Tom made a noise breathing . . . no, he was their mother's, and someone else's, too. When they saw him in town he looked away.

A man smelled different, you felt strange . . . but it would be nice to have a father; Dad had died so long ago he didn't seem true. And he hadn't been an Anzac, Violet Day was nothing to do with him. They just let him get up too soon after the operation for appendicitis. It happened ages ago . . . really, Lou couldn't remember. Who was Tom's dad, then? — Ella only smiled.

Tom watched the birds; he talked to the beetles and King Billy; other times he dug in the sand. His favourite place was on the cliff. Up there, beneath soursobs and quaking grass you found treasure. Tom sat under the she-oak, and counted how many he had. You dug them up, often the wind helped by blowing off sand. They were magic things — shivery-edged blades and scrapers, so smooth; Tom's favourite was the weeny one of milky quartz. King Billy told him what you did. The lagoon in summer, then, used to shrink; you squatted in the mud and spread out your possum and kangaroo skins and rubbed them smooth with your piece of slate. You speared fish off the reef and had a canoe and painted your skin with ochre.

Lou's dreams were different. She wanted knife pleats and *satin de soie*. Oh, Ronald Colman would link her arm, for it was a romance of misunderstood girlhood and the trains came into town, they didn't stop long, as they went on to Melbourne or Adelaide. Well, the former was as far away as heaven, Lou knew there was no chance she'd make it, but the Queen City of the South seemed a cert. Big brother Alfred was there, and the Floating Palais, the *recherché* river rendezvous, too. Also the York, the Wondergraph and West's, where it was your once-in-a-lifetime chance to hear Madame Elsa Stralia sing dramatic soprano from the stage. The *Advertiser* came daily, with mention of the promised land. Anything could happen in Adelaide, the miscellaneous column provided examples: "Young lady in red, dress circle, row F near stairway, Star, Saturday night, care communicate with 'Grey Suit'" ... "A female corrective pill — quick results guaranteed — letters confidential — Sister Rose". In Adelaide there were famous people, you read the same names over and over again: Miss Betty Chenoweth was charming in tinsel pearlette ... Miss Girlie O'Brien and her boy-hero brother foxtrotted at Maison Glenelg ... High society was thrilling, Lou savoured the lovely names, and Tom's breathing faded away: Girlie and Boy, the Misses Cynthia and Kittie Hack ... She always finished off with royalty, though — that way she was sure to sleep sound.

And Queen Mary had daffodil-picking parties at Windsor for the hospitals, but she didn't like the shingle so Princess Arthur of Connaught might have to grow her hair. And the King got a sixteen pound all-Empire cake from the Australian dried fruit growers for his birthday. And Prince George shared the Prince of Wales's penchant for the Florida Club, Prince Henry was tallest, Princess Mary had two little boys. And Princess Betty passed through Kensington Gardens attired in white woollies, but it was sad, for the Duke and Duchess of York would have to leave her. But it was wonderful, too, for they were coming — they were to visit this island continent. The Duchess had a golden Labrador dog called Glen, and did her hair in a Burne-Jones bun.

Lou loved her. There had to be someone. There was Tom, of course, she had him — but Tom was attached to a world of his own. There was Ella, too, but she didn't let you call her Mother. It was more like they were sisters, like Lillian and Dorothy Gish. And: "Ah, it hurts," said Ella. "You never want to have a baby." And you couldn't sleep for worrying about it, but a sister for a mother was good. Lou got a read of the new *True Romance,* and there were feasts of peanut bars and Caramello chocolate. It was a perfect life — you didn't want to lay it on about being like an orphan of the storm. No, for it was a fairy-tale, with Ella smelling of violet talcum, and her leg cocked up interestingly, so you could see all she'd got. Yes, it was good how she lolled on the bed. And if your pillow was dirty — so what? — you could turn it over. Lou knew the trick of rubbing hair off the leg with an emery-paper mitt, and that your lipstick must be the red of your dress, and how a spider weaving downwards meant money to come.

30

And Ella's toe was itchy so it was going to rain, saucer eyes denoted someone selfish, to dream of elephants signified wedlock.

Telling dreams and divining by tea leaves, Ella was nice. And she told secrets, too. About living in the Hills; about running away with Dad and Granpa saying Never come to me for money. But if you tried to tell her a worry, if you said "What will become of me?" and told how you wanted something more — not just the sand and the lagoon for ever — she changed. It was like talking to a stranger; you felt that Ella hated you, then. So usually they were girl friends together; they giggled, they ate the Caramello. When it was time for a visitor, Ella shared the excitement and said "Shall it be the lace or would the crêpe be better?" and then Lou and Tom must hurry away. In winter Ella was considerate: he didn't stay long . . . in any case, a walk on the cliff was bracing; you came back with roses in your cheeks.

Alfred was Lou's other brother. He married Vi and went to live in the city. Vi's dad was someone and now Alf was, too. He had a draper's shop in the Hyde Park Road and the sheets came on the White Star Line from England. Alfred had made himself respectable: Ella reckoned he took after Granpa. Though, really, since Alfred got married he'd stopped being part of the family, even though the card he sent at Christmas said "your loving son". But Ella smirked and said the bugger was too big for his boots. Alfred was having the cash railway put in; he wore French grey trousers, beautifully creased.

Alf wasn't much chop, but when Lou thought of him she felt wistful. She wished he would send for her, take her away from the sand and the town's judging eyes. She saw the other Lou clearly, with a water-wave in her short hair, her shameful body turned boyish. Her bodice wouldn't move immodestly up and down, she'd wear stockings every day . . . anything could happen, anyone might come. There'd be no Tom to spoil her chances (you never knew when he might take a fit, when he'd fall in the road and make the idiot noises). Even better, there'd be no Ella. In Adelaide, Lou would never remember; she'd never even send a card like Alf. It would be as if Ella and her cream-puff body — the crease like a cut between her breasts, the pale blue veins that marbled her legs — had never existed. Lou would never look in the mirror.

But once Ella had been someone else. The little girl who grew up in the Hills was meant for a lady; Gentle Jesus fancied her and Father did, too. She sat on his knee and he plaited her hair, she had lovely hair down to her waist. Remember, remember . . . how you lived in a grand house called Flower Hill, and Mercury stood on one leg in the hall, bronze nigger-boys guarded the stairs. And you went up and up, on and on, till you came to a little wicket gate, and behind it was the nursery, which was where Ella lived . . . her grown-up voice was dreamy as it recalled the rosebud wallpaper and picture-boy Bubbles in green velvet. But, safe upstairs, you longed to be down: Ella played in the garden . . . her voice showed you the lily pond and the frangipani trees with their creamy blooms. But winter always came. The flowers fell like perfumed snow; the creek turned into a river, and one day Ella stood on the rustic bridge and dead animals went by underneath . . . And now her voice told the story so well that, though the child watching the flood was Ella, it was also Lou: and Mother was a tall woman who stood behind you, her embroidery scissors in her hand, and she bent forward, she said:

"Ella, you have nits in your hair," and you saw your shiny plaits tied with satin ribbon float after the bloated cow . . .

"I hated Mother," said Ella, dully. Hated her, hated . . . so much, that Mother caught consumption and Ella turned into a bad girl, the sort that featured as Depravity in the game of Snakes and Ladders. Dolly always took the part of Faith and Obedience, of course; when Doll rattled the dice at parlour games she always had luck.

Aunt Doll was Ella's sister but she was never a child. She was always this freckled creature with ginger hair shedding bobby pins and a tick-tock watch for a heart. "She was never anything to look at," said Ella. "She never got a man." Auntie had been an old maid from birth — always squinting at that fob watch with specs on her nose and a high collar cutting her neck. "Toffy-nosed bitch," said Ella, "looking at me like that — smiling smarmy, pitying me when I came back after Father died." What a laugh. Doll — a scarecrow with paint on her fingers, sticking her tongue out to spit on her sable brushes, hieing away to Dame Nature with sketching bag and roomy camp-stool.

It was only wishy-washy stuff she painted, said Ella. No Spanish galleons on choppy seas or some well-built fellow stripped down. Not even a try at the Virgin in the meadow or St Francis blessing the birds. A realist — lady water-colourist variety, Auntie mostly did eucalypts at evening and early-morning yaccas with a trembly hand. Doll, poor soul, had always lacked imagination. It was only accident and a namby-pamby personality that caused the gum trees to resemble English elms and the yaccas, monster parsnips.

But Ella had shown her what she could do with her

pity. She didn't want a penny of Father's cash. She hated him, as much as she'd hated Mother. Auntie had kept insisting that Ella should have something. Very well then, said Ella, she'd take a few of the old boy's books. What a laugh it was that, all these years after, Tom was the only one who touched them.

And it was real: the sand and the soursobby cliffs, the lagoon with its nests of speckled eggs. But down fell the birds, it was the slaughter of the innocents, and blood dripped from the man's horny hands. The bald coot ate the grass, the swans were torn to pieces, and the swamp and the scrub, the lagoon and the beach with snow bush and salt bush, and the sea that frilled in like a doiley for afternoon tea or spat at the patchwork of little cracked shells — one minute all these things were real, and Lou was emptying sand from her shoe and sweeping the verandah for ever; the next, that world was gone and home became part of a dream.

It started happening when Peg Fox came. Peg was a witch, it was true people said, cross my heart. She had squinty eyes and a droopy nose. She had this shawl darned with black and green spots that made frogs and snakes and jackdaws. But sometimes Peg was Nurse Fox and ladies sent for her, and this day it was for Ella she came — out of her cottage that no one had seen, but there was a hawthorn tree that groaned on Good Friday and arm bones from the churchyard arranged in a star.

Ella was waiting. She'd been crying and the big man's car didn't stop, no buggies came down Parrot Road. Nurse Fox washed her hands and Ella lay on the bed. She had a stone in her belly and veins up her legs. She was ugly, now; Ella's face was old, and Lou knew something terrible would happen.

And, remembering, Ella's blood merged with the birds'. She bled so red; the mattress was soaked. Tom mustn't see, he began to shiver. It was he who went into town. Time ticked away and Lou lit the lamp. The doctor's eyes were scornful. It was too late, he said. "Who did it?" he asked. Hands swooped on Ella and took her away. Sand drifted into the marks of their shoes; soon there'd be no trace that they'd come.

For a while no one told them what to do. Tom hummed as he turned the pages of the encyclopedia, his favourite one stamped B, and full of birds. Lou stirred the soup and they spooned it up. Ella wasn't there to claim her share, but everything else was as usual. Lou said "Wipe your mouth, Tom. Don't tip the bowl towards you."

But next day it seemed true. How Ella was going to have a baby but she didn't want it, so Ella (or was it Baby?) bled away. That day the busybodies came — all the people who ignored them in town. The vicar's wife had an awful taste in hats; Ella would have laughed. She was the one who'd sent the telegram to Alfred, telling that Miss Louise Mundy and Master Thomas would be arriving on the afternoon train.

2

Alfred didn't smile when he met them at the station. But he had a car, and Lou and Tom had never been in one before, and it was the five o'clock rush and people were scurrying: your head kept swivelling, for girls in short skirts were everywhere, and stockings in the city were flesh-coloured not black or white.

They drove down King William Street; Alfred's car smelled expensive, and imagine that he'd ever been Alf, with holes in the elbows of his V-neck. And now they were past the Town Hall; next came Victoria Square, with the dear old Queen on her pedestal. And: "Look," said Tom, "a man with a music box," and they saw a little monkey with a red Turk's cap and a tassel. The monkey was dancing; his collar was studded with brass bells.

In the draper's, Lou dreamed. That Tom was the monkey and Alfred charged twopence for each tune. Alf turned the handle of the music box and "Dance," Vi cried, "You must dance." She had a strap, it came down on Tom's back. "Dance," cried Vi, and then: "Bastard."

Adelaide was a swindle — the part where Lou lived, anyway. The cars that went along Hyde Park Road never stopped; that knock at the door was only a cripple selling shoe laces and boxes of matches.

Though when Lou first saw the shop she felt hopeful. There were high plate glass windows and glittering fittings and an imposing gold-lettered sign. Decidedly, the Bon Marché was a superior establishment: it didn't seem a come-down that Alfred and Vi should live above it.

They didn't enter the shop that day. Instead, Alfred led them through the side door and they climbed the stairs to a drawing room with stuffed furniture and a lady by the veined marble mantelpiece. Her lip stuck out; her pale face went dark when she looked at Tom. She was Vi, and she didn't like them, you could tell straight away.

Their room was bad, too. The stairs kept winding, till everything nice was left behind. Carpet petered out and they walked on scuds of fluff, a daddy-long-legs scuttled up the wall. Then Alfred opened a door and it was an attic; it was full of stuff they didn't want in the shop. As well as the iron bed, there were boxes and show-stands and a group of tailor's dummies with unfashionable bosoms and waists. Most of their heads had come off and stood in a row on a shelf. It was like Bluebeard's chamber. Glassy eyes stared at you, rosebud lips smirked.

Then there was Fish. His real name was Mr Fisher; he looked after Gents' Outfitting and lived in. He was a stumpy man with hairy nostrils who liked to confide. He told Lou that he'd been meant for an academic career; that once he'd been married (the marriage didn't last — it was the problem of sex). Fish rubbed his hands and

37

lowered his voice, and his glasses slipped further down his nose. He wanted Lou to come to his room so he might show her a book.

Each day was the same. Tom must amuse himself in the garden, while Lou sat with Vi in the drawing room. The wireless was on, for Vi was a fiend when it came to listening in. She started with the GPO chimes at half-past ten, then the Studio Orchestra played "Cobweb Castle", and it was time for the serial story. Lou and Vi listened to the running description of the racing at Morphettville, and the "Shipping News" and the "Official Weather Information". There were tenor solos and harp solos and soprano solos. Eventually you reached another set of chimes and close down at eleven o'clock.

While the wireless entertained, Vi liked to talk. She perked up by telling you the worst. Adelaide was ruined now. There were youthful burglars with six-chambered revolvers, and girls couldn't go in for a swim on account of the bestial behaviour of males.

Meals were a trial, too. Fish was always sitting opposite, flaring his nostrils.

But in the shop you needn't see him — as long as you stayed clear of Men's Wear. For, at first Lou was allowed to go in, and she wandered entranced among honeycomb velvets and Fuji silks. But one day Alfred strolled over from Manchester and Lou was ordered out. Alf reckoned she put patrons off. Christmas was coming, the Bon Marché must keep up its style.

But in the new year things would be different. They were going to thin Lou down and cut off her hair. She would like serving. The Bon Marché allowed its girls a discount, and a chair was provided for sit-downs so you didn't get varicose veins.

But Tom would have to go. He was a nuisance, a lar-

rikin element. Boys like Tom did better put away.
Instead of sitting in the garden quietly or making himself
useful by collecting snails in a bucket, he'd begun to dig
a tunnel. Under Alfred's prize tomatoes it went; under
the choko vine and the baby marrows. Why, Tom had
nearly tunnelled under the garden wall — and what was
he doing, was he trying to tunnel out, wasn't he grateful
to them for taking him in? Tom was a disgrace. They
went in fear a customer might know of him. And didn't
he have a trouble? — wasn't there some sort of ail-
ment? It was then Vi said her "Bastard". That night in
the draper's shop, Lou thought again of the little
monkey.

For the shop was too good to stay out of bounds. In
the dark Lou rose from bed and, as Tom slept on, crept
down the stairs and drew back the shop door's bolt. The
moon shone in at the window, though she didn't need
its light: she knew her way by heart, she saw the lovely
things clearly in her head. The smells guided her, too.
The hot damp scent of flannel, the farmyard odour of
corduroy . . . and velvet smelled aristocratic; cotton was
a prim old maid.

Sometimes Lou just stayed in Dress Materials, smelling and thinking of home. The tea-tree round the lagoon
would soon be thick with blossom; as well as ducks,
there'd be swarms of bees . . . And she thought of that
last morning, waiting on the platform for the train —
how Ella's man with the moustache had come up,
embarrassed, and given her the five pound note . . . But
mostly, she thought of Tom and how much they hated
him; and tried to think what she should do. But there
didn't seem to be a solution — thinking could make you
too sad . . . And now here was the drawer that held
sequins and shoe-horn paillettes.

Lou inspected laces and veilings by moonlight; she fingered pure silk hose in shades of Pongee and Nude. In the dark shop she felt happy. She stopped thinking of Tom; about what would happen after Christmas.

And then she got bold — no one would ever know. She went back to Lingerie and chose the Bon Ton corselette and the Royal Worcester for schoolgirls. In the fitting room she switched on the light (it was like magic, so much nicer than an oil lamp) and took off her nightgown.

The Bon Ton had six suspenders and ribbon shoulderstraps; the Worcester was a tight fit . . . but boneless, an elastic gore over the hips . . .

Then Lou felt the hand. It was slithering — first round her schoolgirl waist and then further down. Then, in the mirror, Fish stood behind her. He'd left off his specs and his eyes looked blind; his face was red and somehow blurred. He kept smiling as she hit it.

And she felt cold, but she was sweating, she started to cry. Though Fish was strangely unconcerned. He was a gentleman assistant again, who tutted over the Bon Ton that lay on the floor. It was as if another's hand had done it — he didn't seem to remember.

❦

Christmas for some meant the juvenile panto at the Theatre Royal with its Radiant Ballet of nine; others chose *Mother Goose* at the Majestic or *Puss in Boots* at the Prince of Wales. You could celebrate the season by patronizing Perry's Circus, where Captain Bailey exhibited his posing dogs and Captain Monzalo, the fearless, his tigers and lions. Or view the heroes and bushrangers at the Royal Waxworks and Palace of Won-

40

ders, or motor to Victor Harbour to holiday at Coo-ee or Linga Longa.

Lou pulled a limp cracker with Alfred, and pretended to like her first taste of bubbly, and dodged Fish's questing nostrils. Tom was allowed to pick his turkey bones in peace — Tom was off to the Protestant Boys' Refuge: Tom's fate was settled, he didn't exist. But Lou remained a problem, to be discussed as if she wasn't at table.

Fish thought what was wrong with Lou was green sickness. Girls got it round puberty, he said daringly, savouring the wicked word. It was indicated by a deathly pallor and great lassitude. The spirits were low, the appetite poor, though the body might remain as plump as ever. The disease was a lingering one, and often led on to consumption.

While he helped himself to more brandy sauce, Vi had her say. "Piffle," she said, "there's nothing the matter with the girl." It was Vi who was on the sick list, not Lou. Vi had nervous repression, neuralgia, headache, backache, fidgets and periods of peculiar depression. All that was wrong with Lou was laziness. She took after her mother, she was the living image. Well, the girl would be set to work soon. She was an ungrateful minx. Probably all Lou had was constipation. She needed her bowels manipulated; she ought to eat dates and stewed figs.

And Alfred — what did he say? That it was the big soft woman she missed — Ella, with the dirt between her toes and the musky smell of her body? . . . The tops of her arms were white and wobbly as blancmange, and in summer she always went freckly; in summer, Ella's body reminded you of a milky pudding sprinkled with nutmeg. She worried about the lines round her eyes,

41

and the way her neck was dotted like orange peel. But she was lovely. Running round in her petticoat, the strap done up with the little gold safety pin, her big stomach sticking out. Only she died. Did Alfred remember her at all?

It was hot. After the table was cleared, they went to their rooms for a lie-down. By the coast, summer was different. You could escape the sun in the scrub. The papery rustle of gum leaves was comforting. Leaves and fringes of fallen blossom crusted the earth; there was a dry spicy smell. And Tom always found the orchids — mosquito orchid, onion orchid — in the swamp; it stayed damp there, even in summer. High above your head, the sky was pale, the sun was hazed — the sun had turned into a silkworm's gauzy cocoon. By the coast it tried to trick you, but you escaped it. Beneath the latticed gum leaves, crouched in the cool swamp, or high on the cliff, running through spear-grass. On the cliff you were brave, you leapt at the sky and dared cowardy-custard sun to get you. And there was always the sea — streaming in silvery beads from your body, crowning you with weed . . . Tom liked the sort you could pop, and the queer jellyfish blobs, the rainbow shells . . .

Lou must have slept, for when she woke the room was dark. Night had switched places with day; teatime must be over and she had a nasty taste in her mouth, her head felt full of lemonade bubbles. Dreaming, the old things had felt so near, Ella had been the same as always — in the dream it had been all right to hate her. But now Lou felt choked with an awful melancholy, an unbearable guilt.

It was hot in the room. The waxen heads looked worse than ever; surely those hourglass torsos had advanced while she slept? And then the door opened and of course it was Fish. Lou was dreaming again, and now nightmare began as he sat on the bed.

"Little girl," he said, his voice wobbly with love, his eyes savaging her body. "Pretty pussy," he said, wheedling, and he was the dirty old man who offered the young girl two shillings to go up the lane, and increased it to four when she refused. But he was an academic with a look of scholarly benevolence, he read and read. (Why didn't Lou come and read up his *Manual of Wisdom*, every married person and those about to marry should have one, you got it from the Central Rubber Co. by sending just threepence in stamps?) "Be nice to me, girlie," Fish pleaded. His coat pockets were cut on the slant to the shape of half-moons, braid edged the revers of his waistcoat. "Please," said Fish, and then the nostrils jerked back, the hands let Lou go, for Tom was screaming in the old awful way.

Tom's voice — calling the queer words, keening the secret language — drove Fish from the room. There was just a dent in the bed and the stink of bay-rum to prove he'd been there.

And now Alfred was hitting Tom quiet. He fell back on the bed and Vi said the beast had wet it. The bastard had taken a fit, anything could have happened. He was the child of a dissolute woman; anyone might be his father. Well, he was going. It would be happy new year, 1927. They'd be rid of him as soon as the holiday was over.

The door shut beind them, and Tom lay in that strange stupor that always came after, and Lou smoothed his hair and wiped up the sweat with her hanky. Tom's fit might have been a signal to the sky, for without warning it started to rain. Soon a steady downpour had set in that lasted for hours. Then the wind began — a south-easterly that blew in fitful gusts.

The little room at the top of the Bon Marché seemed like a boat that tossed on a stormy sea. Lou and Tom stayed safe, while outside the window, in a night world turned suddenly cold, roofs blew away from houses and trees fell down. The big hoarding next to the Star Picture Pavilion blew over, the electric lights went out at Henley Beach. Verandahs flew away and telephone posts lay in recumbent positions. People crossed themselves, for God was about. Beans and tomato plants were uprooted; peaches and plums were shaken from trees.

All through the night the storm raged on. Next morning, as church bells rang, one of Alfred's prize plate glass windows was shattered. Vi and he rushed about with dustpans, squabbling as they swept up slivers.

Lou and Tom mostly stayed in the room. Tom read his encyclopedia that told about birds; Lou lay on the bed thinking. After a while she knew what to do. But they couldn't leave yet — as well as being Boxing Day it was Sunday, there weren't any trams.

That night Lou didn't sleep, she was too excited. She woke Tom early, and they crept down the stairs and out the side door with their suitcase. At the tram stop she checked the address again — it was written on the flyleaf of Tom's book.

Granpa was dead, but Aunt Doll must live in his house. How did you get to Fern Gully?

3

When a fit came, a great bird swooped from the beetling cliff: the osprey sped straight as an arrow, like a falling meteor it dropped on the sea. And Tom was that fish it snatched in its gripping talons . . . the fit took him, he was borne from one element into another; he was carried high to be rent piecemeal in a vast sky corral.

But a fit wasn't like that, the doctor said.

But Tom was a reader, he knew. In *The Modern Physician* — after the fold-out man that went from skin to muscle to bone, and the giant insects that walked through your hair — it was featured as Falling Sickness. It started with pains and tinglings, and then the feeling of a ball rising in the throat. You could choose your variety: *Petit mal, Grand mal, Jacksonian* . . . but the doctor shook his head at Ella and said Tom was feigning. "It is hysterics," said Doctor. "The boy is egotistical and craving for sympathy."

Maybe. Perhaps it was like that at first. For, to begin with, it had merely been a game. It had been easy to make one happen. After the ball in the throat there were rainbow lights before your eyes, then blackness. Then Tom fell down and his legs did a grasshopper dance. Though he was careful, he flung himself neatly (he'd never be the awful warning who fell in the fire to be fatally burned). And he stayed comely (there was no saliva froth).

But then the birds started swooping. They got off the pages of the encyclopedia — all sorts: overseas as well as local. The osprey fell on the fish; the raven that presided in gloomy majesty — he made Tom his habitation, too.

For, one day Tom let himself fall but, fallen, he stopped pretending. Suddenly the fit was real, the bird was upon him. It seemed like all birds, every bird . . . with the condor's great wings and the nightjar's gaping beak, the frogmouth's large yellow eye. A bird of hideous aspect flew at Tom, and in his ears was the owl's "boobook", the eagle's piercing cry. But it was Tom. His mouth came open and he spoke, he sang birdlike in the Bible's tongues. And now a paradise bird hung over him: Tom was the centre of a shower of gleaming gold. And then the bird of paradise divided; now Tom's body was pecked all over by the tiny beaks of humming-birds, straight and sharp as needles. They were little marvels. They rose like midget bolts into the sky, flashed upward, sideways, forth and back.

And afterwards he slept for a time, and when he woke he only remembered faintly. It frightened him, he'd wet the bed, but it was also wonderful — what if it never happened again? For Tom didn't know when the birds would take him. It wasn't something you could summon with a blue pill at evening or a teaspoonful of Carlsbad salts in the morning. But it made him afraid, it might be a punishment. Ella had a hat trimmed with egret plumes. The encyclopedia said there were few more harrowing sights than an egret rookery after the depredations of the plume-hunters.

Tom thought of these things as they made for Fern Gully. Even as the tram moved along Hyde Park Road, and the Bon Marché was left further behind, the Gully had become a real place. Granpa's copperplate with the fierce black downstroke had been fleshed out by the conductor's rambling tongue. Fern Gully was up in the Hills, where the south-easterly that blew all last night on the city had come from. You didn't reach it by train, but must travel by charabanc.

Tom and Lou had seen the Hills already. If you stood outside the Bon Marché and looked across the road, you saw them up the end of the street. They were mauvish, mottled with navy; they looked as if they might be made of *papier mâché*. They meant the hill country of the Mount Lofty Ranges that Ella had run from.

Ella had hated the Hills, but she couldn't stop remembering them. Up there grew peaches and apricots, apples and quinces and pears. As well as stringybarks and wattle there were the dwellings of fashionable society — houses that resembled snug castles, with battlemented towers and old English gables, bow windows and sentinel oaks. In the Hills, too, were waterfalls and strawberries and mineral treasures; also jam factories, market-gardens and model nurseries.

When Ella had been a girl, the drive to the Gully often meant the box-seat of a lumbering coach and four. She'd looked down as the River Torrens was crossed, and seen the road begin to zigzag as it climbed. Tom and Lou went the same way, now; they saw the same things, as they travelled by motor charabanc with pneumatic tyres.

All those zigzags were enough to try the nerves of a

timid traveller, but when they reached the summit of the road and looked back, the view provided ample repayment. The Adelaide plains and the waters of Yorke Peninsula lay spread below them like a map.

There were few other passengers. Just a family that alighted in the main street of one of the quiet country villages they passed through; and several maiden ladies of the virtuous sort you didn't really notice; and an old gentleman who sat beside Tom, and appeared to be asleep.

It was wonderful speeding along, savouring the rapid movement through the keen morning air. As they descended, they caught glimpses of water winding through trees. It gleamed polished silver in the sun; it turned purplish as it snaked among shadows.

Yet it seemed to Lou that by travelling to Ella's beginnings she was sealing off her future. She was only fifteen, but nothing could happen to her now. It would be country life for ever, hills in the place of sea, with her smooth body growing wrinkled — and no one to notice, to care.

And though the landscape was stirring, it wasn't the one you were meant to see. The guide-book's Little England was as much a fantasy as that sunset land surveyed by a smiling koala on the patriotic biscuit tin's lid: ivy buds and monthly roses were camouflaged by countless gum trees. And Ella's hating voice had promised green velvet hills. The ones Lou saw now were bleached to the colour of straw.

The rhododendron hedges were dusty. How could you be sure the mansion existed when you couldn't see past the bend in the drive?

But Flower Hill was real, and undoubtedly a house with style . . . and Aunt Doll must be rich . . . and one of

Ella's childhood stories was romantic — about an orchard sloping down to a creek. It was Ella's favourite place, and she never knew if he was somewhere near, furtively watching. For Ella was only a little girl, but there was this man and, truly, he loved her.

Lou believed her; she had the soft look in her eyes that let you know she was really recalling. But then, being Ella, she had to start fibbing. She reckoned the man could make mysterious flowers appear — on the grass, in the creek. Ella fished out the violets before they could drown; next time there were roses dripping with dew in her path.

He was a dandy-looking fellow, quite top-drawer; he was always lurking behind tree trunks. When she ran, he ran too, always keeping to a certain distance. Did she hear him say it, or was it merely the wind in the trees? "Don't run, don't pant," the man said, "it's only your sweetheart behind you."

But nothing happened. He didn't wait for her to grow up. One day in the orchard he whispered goodbye, and there wasn't even time for violets or roses. Doll kept calling that she was to come in to tea. Mama's spy, Doll, had to ruin that last time.

What a pity Ella hadn't run off with him, instead of Dad . . .

"All that was wrong with your father," Ella had said, "was that he was too much of a country bumpkin for Papa's taste." Dad wore his hat on the back of his head; his sleeves were too short, he had a habit of scratching his wrists. "But your dad was a good man," Ella would say. He was a teetotaller, a great talker on platforms.

Which was all right, but unromantic. And didn't account for Alf being a seven month baby.

49

Now the road divided, and one way was Cudlee Creek, the other Fern Gully. All round them were precipitous hills, timbered to the top, with outcrops of rugged crags and in many places a dense undergrowth of gorse. The sun chased them as they drove along, jumping out every so often to surprise them. Suddenly bits of landscape would be lit with gold, in sharp contrast to the shadowy crags.

When they reached the Gully, the town presented a neat and clean appearance. There were several handsome dwellings. By the Post Office was a pebble-dash obelisk that commemorated a local hero who'd died in the Boer War. By the Anglican church a bronze Great War soldier leaned on his rifle.

The charabanc stopped, and the gentleman next to Tom woke with a start. He was a villainous-looking old fellow, grizzly-bearded, with a pale crumpled face and eyes that didn't match — one being boss, the other squinty. The large eye stared at Tom unseeing, like the glass eye of a china poodle, but the little one seemed full of fire — the little eye flicked all over you: Tom felt strange.

Lou distrusted the man straight away. Under the glassy eye forked an angry red scar — something horrid must have happened to him once. And he had a funny smell and wore a droopy hat, green with age . . . yet his threadbare cloak was elegant and flapping. Oh, but he was ugly. He would have done for the Phantom of the Opera. Lou shivered, and the little eye appeared to know her feelings: it snapped at her fiercely.

The old man alighted, too. He grasped a shabby

valise and a queer twisted walking-stick. As the chara-banc started off, he strode away up the Gully Road.

They watched him grow smaller — swinging his bag, shaking his stick at the wind. Tom thought he looked like a mad old bird.

4

And the Duke and Duchess of York were coming, to open the first Parliament at Canberra, and there was to be a special postage stamp and a commemorative florin. H.M.S. *Renown* would bring them (which was the ship that brought the Prince of Smiles in 1920), and it was victualled with a ton of Cambridge sausages, six thousand eggs, two hundred cases of game and poultry, and a quantity of venison from the royal parks. Pheasants had been sent by the King from Sandringham; New Zealand butter would be used throughout the tour. The bed linen was from the royal yacht, and the Duke sent a quantity of silver plate from his London house (the royal party at table would consist of twelve persons; once the tropics were reached all meals would be served cold). There was a squad of marine buglers and a naval hairdresser.

The *Renown*, being of shining silver-grey on the outside (though mostly of blue cretonne within) was known as the Silver Ship. Fittingly, a silver ship sailing on a silver sea would be the centrepiece of Their Highness's dining table, someone having had the inspiration to position there a beautifully wrought model of H.M.S. *Endeavour*, the vessel in which Captain Cook first visited Australia.

The Duchess's prettiness was of the Irish type, and no doubt there'd be an outbreak of fringes, like measles, because she had one. All the evening dresses she'd bring would be of uncrushable velvet, and her favourite colour was cornflower blue (now called Betty blue in her honour). Always, she wore a distinctive fluffy feature, such as a feathery plume in her hat or a soft filmy scarf. And she was married at Glamis Castle in 1923, and then Princess Elizabeth Alexandra Mary was born and christened with water from the River Jordan.

And one day, after a last hug, the Duchess laid the infant princess down, and whispered "God bless my baby", and then the *Renown* steamed out of Portsmouth in a drizzle. The Duke wore naval uniform, the Duchess a dainty costume of dove grey with hat to match. The Earl of Cavan, who was Chief of Staff, had sustained a slight crack of the ankle bone while hunting, and thus had to be carried aboard. He was not expected to regain the full use of his legs till he crossed the line.

They were coming; they'd actually started: "Today the royal ship dropped anchor punctually outside Las Palmas, where a tanker was waiting to oil her for her long Atlantic trip . . . " And the Duchess wore a collar of snow leopard when she landed, and there were worries about the terrors of hand-shaking the Duke must endure (hand-shaking jarred the nervous system of the entire body).

It was all right living at Aunt Doll's. It wasn't Flower Hill, but it would do. "Sorrento" as a house name sounded tasteful, you felt travelled. The newspaper came each morning, so Lou could keep tabs on the royal tour.

Flower Hill had been sold after Granpa died. Auntie had tried to tell Ella it would have to go, but she wouldn't listen. Ella had always believed what she'd wanted to — she had this unshakeable idea that Granpa had died with cash in hand. Times changed. Now Flower Hill was The Frangipani Gardens. And the old de Mole place — that had suffered a change of fortune, too. After the demise of the last de Mole, Gladwish House had been a Methodist rest home; now it was a Roman Catholic school for boys (regularly you saw the scholars in their straw boaters walking in crocodile down the Gully Road). But the jam factory still flourished — had Ella told them about Teakle's? The tea table wouldn't be the same without its pot of choice Teakle plum or fig.

Lou liked Aunt Doll. She was nothing like Ella. She was a small woman, speckly; she made you think of a bantam rooster. Her hair was red — it was a pity she wore it in a bun; her eyes were a pretty blue behind the glasses.

Auntie wasn't anything like an artist should be. She wore the same sort of dresses as Queen Mary; usually in shades of dust or slate. Instead of being wispy, with wooden beads, she was neat as a pin. Disorder annoyed her. The tubes of Windsor & Newton in her studio were laid out in rows, and Auntie got distressed if a screw top came loose. The tips of her sable-hairs were kept licked to exact points — she needed them like that for all her little brush strokes. Dabbing on water-colour, Aunt Doll had a talent for making a subject look embalmed. Her animals appeared to have come straight from the taxidermist; you knew her flowers had never borne relationship to mere dirt. But Auntie's favourite subject was landscape. She was always off roaming the Gully, seeking out bits of England.

Thank goodness she was home when they'd called. After the old man had stalked away, they'd spied a lady outside the Post Office. She'd shaken her head when they'd enquired after Miss Strawbridge of Flower Hill, and directed them to Sorrento.

When she opened the door Auntie seemed to know them — it was almost as if she'd expected them. She listened to Lou's story sympathetically; she wasn't put off by Tom. Fits, doubtful paternity, Ella's image — Aunt Doll could handle them all.

She made their coming seem like a godsend. Lou would help in the house, which meant she'd have more time to paint . . . Tom and school — well, that was a problem they'd face later. Doll took up her writing case, and set about penning a letter to Alfred and Vi.

Sorrento was vaguely Queen Anne; it had terracotta tiles and false gables and rough-cast walls above the bay window. After her childhood home with its ponderous Victoriana, Auntie had wanted something picturesque. Heavy furniture was banished, everything was artistic, with an air of daintiness and grace. Auntie's chairs had spindle legs; her drawing room clock was in the refined Chippendale style.

It was a relief to be with someone calm. Aunt Doll didn't listen to the wireless or entertain gentlemen callers. And after dummies in the attic and sand in your shoe, surely Sorrento was perfect? Flower Hill would have been draughty; Tom might have fallen in the nymphea pond. Lou kept rationalizing as she admired

Auntie's gate-legged table of fumed oak, her milk jug cover edged with beads. But that first day she couldn't help it: she felt disappointed. After the drapery's electric light it was back to candles and oil lamps again. And though Auntie's Aladdin lamp was a beauty, with its incandescent mantle providing a powerful white light — safe and durable and economical — everything about Sorrento was so ordinary; neatness could get on your nerves. Once past that front door inset with a porthole window, nothing was unexpected.

Yet the lavatory swathed in bridesmaid's fern was cosy, with its dangling fly-papers and hessian bag of newspaper squares. You could sit there and see blue sky over the top of the door, and listen to the throaty clucks from the fowl house nearby.

And Sorrento was surrounded by a coprosma hedge, which was also a squeaker hedge (a folded leaf made a whistle if you blew hard). And there was a bush like a lace tablecloth, and a grapevine with a stem as thick as a lady's waist. A crazy-paved path went across the lawn and past the nasturtiums. Beside the quince tree was Auntie's studio.

It had plenty of windows, and some of the panes were coloured. Lou went in, and the sun cast rainbow patterns on the floor. But Auntie's picture on the easel was boring, and the door in the corner, that might lead to something interesting, was locked.

Ella had been right — Aunt Doll was nice, but insipid. She squirmed when she saw a dog cock its leg; she was constantly washing her hands. And the undies went on the clothesline folded, so you shouldn't see their private parts.

5

Autumn, winter, spring — Australia was home. Though
there was a desert somewhere in the centre, it was
nothing to do with you. Blackfellows were there; and
kanga and emu, too, escaped off the coin to run wild.
Some explorers went in after history-book fame, but
you didn't give them much thought. King Billy was only
a ghost; those Abos drinking pinky in Victoria Square
— sitting cross-legged on the lawn with the bronze
queen looking down, and the GPO and Savings Bank so
near — were no relation to the noble savage who could
pick things up with his toes.

Your land was tame and safe. Glenelg, where the
pioneers sailed in, had become the antipodean Deau-
ville. Chic people strolled the silver sands in pyjamas;
there were donkey rides, striped tents. You spread out
your Onkaparinga rug and paddled in your Palm Beach
bathers. The shark alarm bell rang regularly, you kept
applying freckle cream.

But summer could mean a season when you suspected the country to be foreign. For sometimes, out of

the blue, a bad time came and the beach was taboo before dark. Grown men fell down sunstruck, geography maps were blistered on backs. The explorers whose fingernails splintered like glass didn't seem so far away. It was a strange land, savage. Heatwave: and nothing could bring relief.

In January of 1927, the temperature was over the century for six successive days. There was scarcely a breath of wind. Adelaide seemed deserted — people ventured outdoors only when absolutely necessary.

The advent of the iceman was an outstanding occurrence, but even he was bathed in perspiration. The head of the house, in some instances, derived consolation from being able to get hot shaving water direct from the tap. Wise confectioners took perishable wares from their windows, but even so they suffered considerably. Bars of soap and boxes of candles wilted in grocery establishments. The surface of the asphalt highways was often of the consistency of porridge.

Even the delightful zephyrs of a Marelli electric fan couldn't stop you sweltering. Doctors were called to the cots of fretful infants. There were several deaths at the Old Folks' Home and the Salvation Army Sunset Lodge.

Horses showed symptoms of heatstroke; the bird that led in the egg-laying competition conducted by the National Poultry Breeders' Utility Association died. At the Zoological Gardens the carnivorous animals turned up their noses at their usual meat diet. Lions and tigers were affected most, and Miss Siam, the elephant, had a heatwave drink of a hundred gallons, though the polar bears were not greatly perturbed.

In the Hills, the heat had a serious effect on orchards and fruit gardens. There'd been a fair crop of Cleopatra apples, but the greater portion was now burned. Plums were prematurely softened, green figs were scorched; the apricot crop was finished somewhat abruptly by the fruit being more or less melted. Peaches had not fared so badly, as the trees carried dense foliage.

Most of the gardeners had their own water supplies, obtained from wells, bores and creeks. The water shortage, felt acutely in the suburbs, did not affect them. Sprinklers played on cabbages, turnips, potatoes and peas. In the moister parts of Fern Gully, rapid growth was made by sun-loving plants, particularly melons, tomatoes and sweet-corn.

Beyond the blind, Aunt Doll's garden blazed in the sun. Everthing was tipped with points of light. The garden had become a danger zone by day: you must keep inside Sorrento while the sun did its worst. You sat in your singlet, your petticoat; you flapped with Fiji fan and stuck cucumber peel to your forehead. The garden was forbidden until the sun plummeted earthward and the hard blue sky was softened by night.

But it was tiresome to be confined indoors while light beckoned from under the blind, and you knew that outside was shimmering brilliance and the challenge of furnace heat. Sorrento had taken on the aspects of a dim underworld place, as it did battle with the blinds, the lowered windows. Yet summer still filtered in. Tom longed for the garden. Auntie's house reduced the dashing sun to something as smally irksome as the itch in your flannel underwear, the pinch in your Sunday boots. Housebound, the summer was a thick cocoon and you were lost in it; it wrapped you in mummy bandages, you would never get out.

Lou was content, stitching at the fancy dress she must have — then abandoning her lapful of tulle to stare pensively into the mirror (staring in mirrors, dreaming, seemed Lou's favourite occupation since she'd made her new friend); Auntie was engrossed before her easel. But Tom would go crazy if he didn't escape. Outside were rock pebbler parrots and finches, plumed pigeons and Alexandra parakeets . . .

It was an adventure from the start. The magpies gurgled, gargled; and there was another bird — a stranger Tom couldn't place — that trilled invitingly; that seemed always hidden somewhere ahead.

It was the unknown bird's teasing tra-la that lured him on. Past the intensities of marigold and lobelia and the deep purples of Auntie's lantana. By the lantana bush Tom was encircled by a host of amber-winged butterflies, and then he was out of the light; the bird led him on under Auntie's snaking grapevine and he was dappled with shade. The grapes hung like pendant marbles; the zigzag leaves moved languidly, and a series of fragmented shadow leaves moved, too. There were corkscrew tendrils and the dotted remnants of last year's Lady's Fingers. And then the sun pounced again, and here was Auntie's prize hydrangea, hidden from the sun inside a little house of sacking. And then Tom was even past the squeaker hedge, now he was out in the lane.

Bleached grass leaned forward stilly, as if bewitched by the heat; there were pussy-tails, dandelions. It was strange what summer could do. The earth was pelted in creamy plumes and stubble; the gum trees came alive with shiny new leaves and nuts and blossom . . . some leaves were blunt and pale; others resembled dusky sickle moons . . . But you grew tired of screwing your eyes at the sun, so Tom looked down and let his eyes tag his feet. It was surprising how much you saw from a blinkered viewpoint. The weeds and fallen leaves; occasionally an ancient dog turd, whitened and crumbly.

Tom had been walking for ages, now; he'd gone so far he'd walked the lane away: it petered out before a high grassy bank. And Tom clambered up it, and then he was going down — slithering, sliding over a tangle of brambles and ivy.

He came to a creek edged with willows, and he took his shoes off and started to paddle. The creek ran so clearly that every pebble and leaf beneath its surface might be seen. There were tadpoles and mysterious splashes, and still Tom heard the bird that had led him to the perfect place.

But, soon, instead of willows there were eucalypts and the creek had shrunk to a mere trickle, the pebbles he trod had stopped being smooth. Yes, the pebbles were the first things that started to be odd — though Tom felt peculiar, too. For it was the strangest feeling, it was as if the creek tried to frighten him away. For, instead of being smooth and dead, the pebbles looked alive. Some stones had the faces of animals and the fox tried to get Tom with its tongue, the rat bared its teeth.

And he knew he was meant to turn back, but he wouldn't. No, for it was an adventure, but the animals kept nipping and nuzzling — they did it fiercer, now, and he looked down and saw, wedged between two of their muzzles, a little clay man. Tom knew he was meant to pick him up.

The real world swirled back: smooth dead stone and silvery water and now and then a tadpole flickering. Tom held the clay man, and saw he was stabbed with pins. Without knowing why, he knew he must draw them out.

61

After he did it, he felt afraid. The gum trees stretched up to reach leaves and wild winds and the mad mutter of flies, but there was only a terrible silence. Then out of it came the song of the strange bird that had teased him from Auntie's garden. It sang louder and more taunting than ever, and Tom looked up and over his head it came swooping — the biggest bird he had ever seen.

It was fantastic, a grim creature of night — stealthy, soft-flighted. It was a pair of wings threateningly drooped, two eyes glaring as with fire, a cruel lusty beak. Tom flinched as the great shadow fell upon him; he cried out, and even his cry was a cheat, for once free of his mouth it changed tune, it swelled on the air till it sounded as if every tree sang. The willows he'd left behind, the gums that had taken their place. And everything else. For the whole landscape — the creek and its banks and the sky — seemed to shout. There were shrieks and squawks, occasional warblings, sounds as of tearing calico. And still the strange bird hovered, it fanned him with its sinister wings. But Tom held the clay man, perhaps it was a charm that would help him; so he held it tighter, he looked at it: and it was awful. For the manikin had somehow become the bird in the sky. The bird had fallen down, it had got Tom at last, but it wasn't giant-size at all. It was a tiny thing: a bird — but pink, featherless, defenceless. Cradled in Tom's hand, on its back with its rubber legs jerking and its yellow beak gaping, gagging on air. It had eyes like jelly; its bald baby head was studded with specks — like black-heads, like little black pins stuck in.

And then perhaps he died, for it was another world when he woke up. Instead of a bird, there was a dog. Big and soft and gentle; honey-coloured, with a stomach like a barrel . . . but it was mostly a mouth, that drooled and lapped and mourned. Poor Tom. Possibly it wasn't death but a fit. A fit always meant birds. Though unlike the one he'd lately seen. And Tom shut his eyes, in case the horror might still be there. Somewhere, far off, the dog bewailed him.

Then he was a lump of meat and the butcher had him. Hands, scratchy as fig leaves, lifted him high in the air, he was slung over someone's smelly shoulder. There was a thumping in his head; he felt like a sacrifice to the sun. And then there was shadow, green shade. The old man from the charabanc set him down under the willows.

They sat together on the grass and looked each other over. Again, the man made Tom feel different — stronger, somehow powerful, as if he wasn't merely a child. For a while he tried to grapple with the feeling, to understand it . . . But thinking was too hard: Tom stopped, and the man sitting beside him relaxed. His beard ceased trembling, his little fierce eye gave up its blink.

He didn't seem ugly now. His face was wonderfully interesting. The large eye was certainly glass . . . how had he come by that scar?

Gravely, they exchanged names. The man was Charlie Roche, and you didn't have to call him Mister; the dog answered to Caesar.

At the lagoon, there'd sometimes been tramps. They'd worn the same rag-bag assortment of clothes as Charlie; they'd had beards and a smell. But up close they were ordinary men, understandable, as they cadged tobacco or a bed for the night. There was a strangeness about Charlie. He reminded Tom of an Old Testament prophet who talked in tongues and flourished his staff at burning bushes.

But Charlie only had a walking-stick and he spoke

English, though in a peculiar way. Despite bearing no resemblance to Johnnie Chinaman who pushed the laundry basket or the Italian who wanted to sharpen your knives, his accent sounded as foreign. He didn't talk Australian, his voice sounded like music.

Charlie was comforting. Sitting beside him, you knew that the small tight worlds people sought to imprison you in had no power. For once, here was a person who couldn't be neatly labelled, diminished to fit a certain pigeonhole of class or creed. He had the cheek to be an original, to flaunt an inconvenient hugger-mugger of styles. Before Charlie and his unruly hair and ravaged face, his workman's hands and musical voice, the small safe worlds lost their threat.

Yet Tom was used to being alone. By himself, he could read and summon up King Billy; he had the birds and his fits. He wasn't like Ella, needing another body for company; he didn't sit dreaming of royalty, like Lou. Not even Vi nor Alfred nor thought of the Protestant Boys' Refuge could cast Tom down for long. Always, he'd felt assured of a last minute reprieve. It was shaming, then, that a clay doll should have upset him so much; that a fit — a familiar nasty-nice occurrence — had left him cowering, and a bird had been transformed into the thing he feared most. Tom had seen countless unfledged birds at the lagoon.

But as he'd waded in the creek, when he'd pulled the pins from the manikin, everything had turned topsy-turvy. The earth had seemed haunted, unreal. Tom shivered, even though it was a record heatwave day. He wished he'd stayed in the dark at Sorrento. Against his will, he'd been propelled into a nightmare world.

But the bad time was past — perhaps it had never happened. He sat beside Charlie under the willows; the creek ran blithely over pebbles that bore no resemblance to animals; there was no clay man, no bird.

But it was no use pretending. Something had happened to him — something he didn't understand — and everything was changed.

For Tom felt now as if he hated birds; for a bird — the thing he'd loved most — had betrayed him, had hurt him more than even Ella's dying, had proved crueller than the tongues of the ladies who'd whispered about him in town. For the first time in his life Tom hated. He wished he was the man who had ruined the lagoon with his gun. He wanted to shoot down ducks, pelt swans with stones, plunder the sparrow's nest.

6

And the *Renown* had passed Jamaica and Panama, and now it was Crossing the Line. Neptune invested the Duke with the Order of the Skippered Sardine; the Duchess was appointed Mistress of Mermaids, Sea Nymphs and All Such by Amphritite, his consort. The Earl of Cavan was made a General of the Horse Marine. At the request of the Duke, the mainbrace was spliced and tots of rum were served all round.

And in Adelaide, citizens met in the Mayor's Parlour to hear the joint report of the Decorations and Illuminations Committee. It was decided that King William Street should be garlanded with gum leaves; that Victoria Square would feature columns similar to those erected to the Caesars in Rome.

And in the Hills, the hot spell was over. Summer rains had fallen, filling empty water-tanks and freshening the country.

Young grass was springing up everywhere, and the pear crop was likely to be heavy, and everything seemed right with the world. The *Renown* was making for the Marquesas Islands; Lou had a special friend.

It had been a day before the heatwave. Lou was exploring the orchard when a lady came towards her. She was tiny, like a Japanese doll, with enamelled hair and porcelain skin. And she lowered her sunshade and smiled, and turned into someone familiar. For it was Girlie O'Brien, and Lou read of her on the social page regularly. It seemed natural they should be talking together. But it was unbelievable, too. Who'd imagine they should become friends at sight; that each day after that, Lou should take the short cut through the orchard to the model nursery.

And you walked between the apple trees and came to a wooden gate (nothing could be more different to the fancy iron one that barred your way at the front). And painted on the flaking wood you could still make out that faint FLOWER HILL.

But the old name meant nothing to Lou, now. She visited The Frangipani Gardens: it was Girlie's home. Since meeting her, the fact that Auntie and Ella had lived there before her, had faded away. Frangipani trees and rustic bridge had meaning, now, only because Girlie saw them constantly. There were servants and an acetylene gas generator. Everything was so impressive that it was easier, more convenient, to imagine the place to have been O'Brien-owned from its inception.

Girlie's papa was a stage Irishman with a yappy voice. The boy-hero was a melancholy man.

It seemed unlikely that Mr O'Brien should possess a mama, but he did. Gran, poor soul, turned giddy when she stood, so must sit all day. She was wrinkled as a dried fruit; her veined hands were specked with age marks. But Gran, despite her ancient body, wasn't worn out in spirit. You only said the "poor" automatically. She wasn't a nice old lady by any means; she stayed nasty and indomitable with a Clara Bow mouth.

But they should have sat her in another room. The one she was in had been a nursery — Lou knew that little wicket gate on the landing; those faded wallpaper rosebuds.

The room was all wrong. Ella's past mocked Lou's present. Strawbridges had lived here once; The Frangipani Gardens had been Flower Hill.

Though you only caught glimpses of wallpaper, for there was a forest of pot plants, and the holy pictures blocked out the bits that fern fronds didn't hide. Blood fell in dewdrops from Jesus' thorny crown; a host of saints clasped lily stalks as they endured impossible tortures.

Granma had visitors when they went up to see her: two Christian Brothers who put down their teacups while Girlie introduced them. "Brother Keogh," she said, "Brother Wells." And one faded into the gloom of the room, he wasn't as real as the plants or the saints on the wall. But the other, Brother Wells, stood out. He had a face like a gargoyle; he had watery eyes, and the folds underneath reminded you of bat's wings. And his nose was a snout with tight nostrils, but he had loose lips — the lower was so swelling, it cast such a shadow, that it seemed he had a scab on his chin. And he had black hair brindled with grey, and was red round the mouth . . . perhaps he shaved very close; perhaps it was caused by his rubbing. For, all the time he talked he did it — rubbed his mouth with his hand, so that the words sniggered out through his fingers, so that everything he said sounded secret. His hands were long and white. When he wasn't talking, his fingers moved in his lap. Lou watched them latticing, making steeples.

Where Brother Keogh looked merely dusty, the other was beautifully got up. If you skipped his face, Brother

Wells was a dandy: his tab-cat hair sticky with pomade, the scurf brushed away from his shoulders; his priest's dress fitting above waist like a skin, to flare to a missish skirt. The beads round his neck glistened; ditto the silver cross with its little writhing man.

Gran's companion, Pearl Reed, came in for the tea things. With her pale hair and skin, and the curiously frosted shadows round her eyes, she resembled some original variety of Snow Queen.

Lou felt uncomfortable — she had a feeling Pearl disliked her. She was glad to leave Granma and the Brothers, and follow Girlie down the stairs.

A *bal masque* was to be held at the Floating Palais. It was the Fig Leaf Ball, and the name was adopted from the motion picture *Fig Leaves*, which was the coming attraction at the Wondergraph. Girlie had the tickets already and Lou was invited to attend. Fancy dress might be worn as well as masks; there'd be a fashion parade and an Adam and Eve contest.

There was a letter in the newspaper from "Deeply Concerned" urging Christian parents in the City of Churches to protest against the proposed demoralizing exhibition of youths and maidens (leopard skin and fig leaves were degrading; even on the Continent it wouldn't be allowed). But the manager of the Floating Palais wrote in to say that the Adam and Eve costumes were being made by a well-known Adelaide firm. Of heavy imitation leopard skin worn over trunks, they were a modern adaptation, both modest and graceful, of the costume of an ancient day. The Floating Palais was a high-class dancing resort. "Fig Leaf" was used more with the object of inspiring fun than suggesting anything risqué.

All through the heatwave, Lou sewed her costume. Left to herself, she would have chosen something dashing — perhaps the Queen of the Amazons in a tiger-skin bodice. But Girlie took charge, and said Lou should take advantage of her old-fashioned looks. She narrowed her eyes and mused . . . Yes, she had it: Lou would make a striking Last Rose of Summer, and Girlie would supply the tulle that would do the trick.

At last it was the night of the Ball. The pink tulle, with its elbow sleeves and ruffles, suited perfectly, as did the wreath of roses in her hair. Auntie said it was like seeing Ella again. Lou went through the orchard feeling excited, strange. She had turned into someone beautiful.

Girlie was a Child of the Dawn in a frock of green chiffon besprinkled with glittering beads that resembled dewdrops. Boy was a dandy in tails and white tie, with crystal links at his cuffs and a carnation in his lapel.

The Dodge waited in the drive. Girlie just had to pick up her half-moon shawl and they'd be off.

But time ticked on. Lou was the Last Rose, but she felt like the Invisible Girl. The O'Briens ignored her — they were engrossed in a game of cards. It wasn't Fish or Snap. Girlie turned the card over and a thunderbolt chopped the top off the pyramid. And the maiden had her hand in the lion's mouth; the hanging man's hair touched earth.

It was only cards — only a game, but they played as if they took it seriously. Boy sucked his mouth in, he concentrated so hard that his face was mazed with lines; Girlie's cheeks were on fire as her hands revealed Enchantress and Martyr, but her voice was ice-cold. The

Child of the Dawn sat in the drawing room, but really she was far away. Girlie was out of Lou's reach. It was the drawing room — it was a land of perpetual snow . . . there were ice-caverns, brittle glaciers, frozen seas.

But, not so long ago, apples had baked on trees, apricots collapsed and grapevines were scorched. It had been hot, very hot, and Sorrento was an oven with every blind drawn, but Lou stayed inside, squinting as she sewed at her dress. Aunt Doll went out in the garden and came back with a lobster face, the sun climbed higher in a cloudless sky, but Lou's needle kept flying, she kept pricking her fingers, but the stitches went on. For the dress was for Girlie as much as for Lou — oh, how she missed her friend. The earth was cracked like elephant skin; hatpins turned fiery; old people were dying, babies, too, and Lou dreamed of Girlie. Then a change came. Cooler conditions were ushered in by a westerly breeze which gradually gained in strength. And the dress got finished, rain fell, and the pomegranate flowers would soon be lacquered red fruit. And, dreaming, Girlie merged with the Duchess: the *Renown* came closer across the Pacific; a doll-like being waved from the rail . . . Sometimes, when she awoke, Lou felt afraid. It would be awful if Girlie cast her aside.

But the Tarot cards had been gathered up, now; Boy's fate was shut away in a box. Girlie's voice was cooing, coquettish as it complimented the Last Rose on her dress.

Yet still they didn't start off. Girlie sighed and said she wished he'd come.

But when the door opened it looked like a girl. A skinny creature minced in, so proud of her silk jumper suit, her matching Lenglen bandeau. The O'Briens stared, as if they didn't know her. Then Girlie started to laugh.

The smart girl was a man. They introduced him as Swells. He was a horror, with his fuchsia mouth, his primrose hair; yet he had the nerve — despite the pin-prick shave dots showing through the powder, the half-plucked hairs like tacking threads under his eyebrows — to make you feel small.

Silent secret laughter was everywhere. It was a lark, a giggle, and Boy and Girlie and Swells — despite occupying separate chairs — were linked together, tight-clenched. Lou was left out as their smoke-screen words said one thing; as their smirks and side glances said another.

First they talked about the Tarot cards, and: "Devil cards," sniggered Swells. "Naughty, naughty." And he said he was dying for an outing in the wicked city, and the boarders were back already — it would soon be copybooks and inkwells again. And it had been simply ages since he'd broken bounds — last time had been for Greta Garbo in *The Torrent*. And Dame Gossip wondered how Girlie was progressing with her new little friend; and wasn't Boy's profile just too Valentino; and didn't they fancy Swells's ensemble, wasn't his toilette divine? And all the time he talked, his hands kept rubbing — if Swells wasn't careful he'd rub off the make-up, and who would he be then?

And now Brother Wells was sipping a Manhattan, he was smoking a miniature cigarette. And cocktail glasses were elegant; maraschino cherries, delightfully red — Lou felt more alone than ever as she drank lemonade. They were sophisticates, playing a game of pretending, with smoke coming out of their nostrils.

And then the car swerved, for Boy was momentarily blinded by the sun. It hung before them, luminous orange — gleaming, glistening, raying out. The sun seemed to dance, and below it lay a pastel-pink city . . . and that haze was the sea. Lou's eyes watered, she blinked: tiny mauve suns danced like confetti across the windscreen, and the suburbs lay before them, sober, pearl-grey. Then they took another bend and the real sun came back, but so changed. Now it floated diminished on the ocean; now, reflected, the sun duplicated itself to form a pair of lips. Then, in a last pout of orange, it disappeared — the sea sucked the sun away.

It was dark when they left the car and joined the gay throng, masked like themselves, who made for the Torrens. In the daytime, this part of the river was where you ate your lunch from a paper bag and pelted seagulls with sandwich crumbs and hummed in tune to the band that played from the rotunda. With evening, everything was different. The river bank had turned into the badlands of Pinky Flat, and an army of ragged metho-drinkers who stayed hidden by day stationed themselves under the poplars to pass round bottles and curse the moon. And voyeurs crept through the reeds; and sometimes a typist in an incipient condition tried to drown herself; and, always — up by the University Bridge, down by the weir — the lovers pressed closer together and ignored the sounds of departing last trains and the chiding voice of the GPO clock. But tonight was a dance night — the derelicts were tidied away, the trees hung with Chinese lanterns. Love stayed decorous and fairy-fingered, as you circled to the "Floating Palais Waltz".

And yet it was merely a dance hall built on a raft moored against the river's south bank — only a structure of flimsy wood with a little picket fence round the promenade deck . . . but crowned with several fanciful domes, reminiscent of Baghdad, City of Delight.

There was a crowd of sightseers gathered round the gangway, on the chance of seeing something shameful. Lou went past them on to the barge, and wished she wasn't partnered by Swells.

For, in public, Girlie and Boy were a pair. They walked side by side like husband and wife; they sat with elbows touching. Now they were out on the dance floor, one-stepping briskly with fixed smiles.

Left with Lou, the Christian Brother didn't bother to be amusing. He slumped in his chair, drawing moodily on his cigarette. His lurid mouth drooped; he twitched at his skirt with restless fingers. Lou wished more than ever that she wasn't fated to sit out the evening with this gawky half-thing beside her.

But the big sliding windows were open to the night and it was romantic: the river beneath you, the stars coming close. The swinging opal lamps were wreathed in sweet peas; you sat on a gilt chair and, as the Palais Syncopating Melodists played latest tunes, watched Spanish dancers and Eastern princes, Christy minstrels and a clever set of Pierrots with whitened faces.

Lou admired fringes and feathers, petalled skirts and handkerchief-point hems. The ladies danced, and a shimmer of bugle beads and glitter-glass, sequins and diamanté danced, too. Chiffon roses and delicate orchids bloomed on shoulder-straps; there were pearls like pigeon's eggs, diamonds like threepenny pieces; bracelets inset with lapis, cornelian, sapphire.

Watching the dancing, Lou forgot Swells. She could

smile when Girlie and Boy came back, and they went up on the roof where *Fig Leaves* was being continuously screened.

It was the sensation of the cinema season, gripping in its interest. All about woman's craving for adornment through the ages. Eve and the modern flapper . . . the same old tale: I haven't a rag to wear . . .

They came down in time for the fashion parade of My Lady's Wardrobe, during which Miss 1927 gave a dissertation on the evolution of dress, and "Emancipation" appeared swathed in black, which was wound off her to reveal white silk tights trimmed with flowers and leaves (she made her exit in a scarlet shawl). Then came the couples in their leopard skins; then the band started up a Charleston, and Girlie laughed rougishly as she manoeuvred Swells forward to partner Boy.

And, for an instant, Lou saw the boy-hero as he must have looked on the battlefield. His face was grim as he pushed the Christian Brother away. People were staring; the white-faced Pierrots edged closer. They giggled softly as Swells reeled back. There was hate on Boy's face as he seized Girlie's wrist and dragged her out on the floor.

They were Charlestoning, and all the Roman Catholic Bishop of Derry said in his Lenten pastoral was true. For the Charleston as Girlie and Boy did it, was a mad bad dance — an open incentive to passion, immodest, freakish and negroid.

Now they clung together; now they drifted apart to turn and kick out dangerously. They were ardent show-offs with supple knees. Girlie's dress rippled in beaded shivers; Boy's teeth were bared as he clasped her to his piqué chest, then flung her away.

The floor was crowded, but they danced within a

small space. The other couples' movements appeared awkward, arthritic. The band played loudly, but it couldn't disguise the silence that had swept the ballroom. Heads were shaken meaningfully; eyebrows raised.

It was a war they danced out on the floor. Yet, when the music jerked to a halt, their passion seemed spent. For a moment their masked eyes were bewildered, they smiled dreamily. By the time they returned, they were as coldly indifferent as ever.

It was hard to believe, as they small-talked lightly, that it had happened. But Swells was decidedly sulky and the Pierrots still eyed him with interest.

There were four of them. They all had the same chalky faces and loose white calico costumes with a row of black pompons down the front. But one had lost his conical hat: this Pierrot was Lou's favourite. He had a cheeky grin and a mop of curly blond hair.

And now, as the band played a waltz, a flood of softly-shaded light fell on the dancers. Now they were covered with a rosy mist; then blue shadows touched them gently. And suddenly Girlie was Lou's friend — she noticed her; she smiled affectionately, kindly, and said it was her turn to dance. Boy rose to take her arm, and then, as the amethyst light changed to pink, Lou was dancing — but not with Boy.

For a figure in white seized her, and they skimmed over the polished floor. It was blissful. Waltzing with Pierrot, Lou couldn't stop smiling.

He wasn't Valentino; you could never imagine him rescuing you from the fog-bound London underworld. His hair was a mop of curls, he had a comical nose. Lou wished he didn't wear a mask. She suspected he was only a boy, not much older than herself.

And then she saw Girlie watching them: Girlie danced closer with Swells. They were an ill-matched pair — the pantomime dame stooped over the elusive Child of the Dawn. Then, cursing as his high heels faltered, Brother Wells swung Girlie round: now it was he who stared suspiciously at Pierrot.

And the band played louder and faster, and balloons, like rainbow-coloured bubbles, showered down from the ceiling. It was midnight, and Pierrot ran across the ballroom with a rose he'd plucked from Lou's hair.

On the barge's roof the motion picture started again. A demure Eve selected her fig leaf; a wily serpent whispered temptations.

7

Anything could frighten Tom now — even the cedar chest in Aunt Doll's hall. To begin with, though — before he looked inside — it was merely something to admire. It had carving on its lid and splendid brass clasps: you could pretend it held Spanish doubloons.

But once it had been Auntie's glory box, her hope chest, filled with doilies and tablecloths and night-gowns. Only Auntie was never a bride. The nighties stayed folded away in tissue paper; the linen was made everyday with iron-mould, without even a hint of romance. Now the chest was mostly full of photos.

They were of all the lives that had gone before. Tom opened the chest and breathed in the mingled scent of camphor and cedar . . . and here was Granpa in the footer team, the best of the lot, with muscles in his arms and a wave in his hair. And he stood there for ever and ever, but the timekeeper held out his watch: Granpa got married. Then, there he was with Gran — she, so shy, maidenly, with this terrible soft face she ought to hide, and the roses in her hands a bit trembly, for when the

down the slope to the factory. Tom watched for a bit, and then walked further along the road.

And then he wished he'd never left Sorrento, for he saw a girl who was just a shell of flesh. Her spirit had flown away, she was empty inside. She lay on the ground like a small forest animal; she slept among the leaves and grass.

She was a dead girl, though she breathed with little puffs. And now she saw Tom — she opened her haunted eyes, she bit at her poor pale lips. Her hands were grubbing in the dirt, as if they sought some object she loved.

Tom was afraid. She was a girl like Lou, but she squirmed on the earth in her nightie. Tom ran away from her, and Cockroach caught him.

But his hands were gentle. He was the devil who made lily tongues poisonous; spittlebug on blackberry leaves was cast by his mouth. But his fingernails were cut short; there were no fleas in his beard. Girlie had lied. It wasn't Cockroach, but Charlie.

The robin made his nest of moss and leaves, and hid it away in the ivy bush. The jackdaw preferred high towers; the rook chose the tallest tree. The jay gave a scream when intruders approached and flew to the heart of the wood. And Charlie Roche was a hermit who'd concealed his hermitage as cunningly as any bird. To reach it you must get down low; you must trip and slide and stumble.

But at first it was easy going. Tom and Charlie walked through an orchard that differed from the usual Gully variety, in being old and abandoned. It had deteriorated into a neglected wilderness, which meant that

besides apple trees there were all sorts of weeds and herbs and flowers. Butterflies zigzagged crazily, everything blistered and shimmered in the early morning glare. Then the ground dipped, and leaf patterns arched above them.

Now the path was narrow, the grass tickled Tom's chin; now they were deep in a jungle of blackberries and thistles. And here and there were coils of barbed wire — it was like crossing a battle zone, for next came trenches and traps and earthworks, and a tunnel you negotiated at a crawl.

Tom might have been back at the lagoon, crawling through the tea-tree. But this was better, for you kept being surprised. You blundered into a cat's cradle of wire and a bell rang; you emerged to confront a remarkable defence line. After the tunnel was the army of wild bees.

They walked across the clearing towards the hermitage. All about it was Charlie's garden. It seemed to be planted with weeds. Though, as they drew closer, Tom saw that the bushes were herbs. He'd never considered before how many different greens there were . . . and each variety of leaf had a shape of its own; each leaf smelled different when you plucked and pinched with your fingers. Sage was grey and smelled greasy; the dark green needles of rosemary were cough-mixture spicy; mint was so pungent it made your mouth water.

Charlie's house resembled a log cabin. Inside, the walls were lined with wheat bags, painted whitish with lime and cement. The floor was a patchwork of stones.

There was just one big room, interestingly muddled with books and bunches of dried herbs and shelves of bottles and jars. The room had the same smells as the

garden. Charlie's bed was spick and span in a corner; there was a colonial oven, the sort with iron bars standing on bricks, and a fire in the top part to boil your kettle on.

A camp oven was an iron pot with legs and a lid — Charlie had one of those, too. He kept his food in a Coolgardie safe.

But the best things were up on the wall. Tom remembered the travelling circus that had the Woolly Woman of Hayti. Well, Charlie didn't own her, but the Jap Mermaid and the Nondescript were as good.

They were perfectly hideous, Tom felt wonderfully happy. It had been another boy who'd flinched from a slug.

The Mermaid's head and body were those of a small monkey with prominent teeth; below the ribs the skin of a carp was so neatly joined that it was hardly possible to detect where fish began and monkey left off. The villainous Nondescript was mostly composed of cedar, with *papier mâché* overlay, artfully applied in wrinkles, admirably coloured.

Tom left off looking, for Charlie had called him. Charlie was holding out his hand, and in it lay this other pretend thing.

But the clay doll was part of a dream. Tom was content — he refused to remember. But, standing in Charlie's room he felt he was somewhere else. He was alone in Auntie's garden, lured from Sorrento by the dashing sun. And then he heard a little singer — it was always ahead, lurking in hiding, enticing him on. And, by the creek, the bird ceased being a shy garden warbler — cheerful chiff-chaff or neat willow wren. Instead, it was fierce and pitiless as a tiger or a volcano; it was a bird of battle, a feathered emblem of destruction. And it fixed

Tom with its telescope eye: Tom was changed to a rigid statue of himself. It was a fabulous monster of old belief — harpy eagle, Sinbad's roc; it was a fallen unfledged nestling . . .

It was merely a doll, but it had power, and something awful would happen because Charlie held it. But it didn't. Charlie was smiling. He moved towards Tom, he took his hand. Now it was Tom who held the clay doll — and nothing happened.

For the manikin was as much a hoax as the Japanese Mermaid. Charlie began to talk. His voice talked away Tom's fear.

Sun came in at the window; Caesar wagged his tail. It was but a child's plaything. Despite all the pin-pricks. For that was true, too — the part where Tom pulled out the pins. But why had they been there, who'd pushed them in?

Charlie told Tom that the clay image was nothing to fear. It had power, yes, but its power only worked against you when you were lost, lonely, afraid — when you'd had a touch too much of the sun. But Tom knew, didn't he, that he had a far more potent strength of his own?

And yet he was weak, a child, he had the fits. Wandering through the scrub, conversing with King Billy, fingering his pieces of quartz, reading — always reading, were sure signs of incipient madness. The big boys in town had despised him. They stopped up their noses when he went past (TOM MUNDY STINKS was chalked on the grocery wall beside the Rosella sauce parakeet). They bit their thumbs at him; they pelted and spat and tripped him up. And one day the tea-tree was full of them; they were hunting him, as the man with the gun hunted birds. Everything familiar went dizzy with fear; Tom felt sick as they hedged him closer. Then it was the circus and he must stand on his head, he must hang from branches. And they fought him with sticks; they caught him and took off his clothes. He stood before them shivering and they pinched him, they stuck in their sticks to see if he was real. He was a zombie, they said, because of a voodoo curse.

Charlie called him a Troubadour of God. It was like seeing with magic spectacles: Charlie had seen from the first that Tom was a fellow traveller. They were pilgrims, dwelling among a foreign race. They spoke the same language; they saw alike, felt alike. And the devil and the world looked at them angrily, they would always desire to strike and smite them. But there were guardian angels to preserve and protect against all dangers. And, in the end, nothing was unexpected. You counted wounds and prison, torture and death among God's gifts.

But the clay man . . . It had been made by someone in the Gully who was sick; a dabbler in esoterics — someone who'd started off pondering tea leaf patterns and gone on to easy lessons in dream interpretation and how to rule the stars. Mysticism was chic. It gave you an uplift as enjoyable as a Martini cocktail or a sniff at a Blackboy rose. It was something to do with gipsy bangles and incense sticks, the Curse of Tut and eating bean sprouts. And Lord Wavertree would do no yachting this year because his horoscope proclaimed a season of hurricanes; Armageddon was fast approaching — you had the date deduced from Biblical prophesies and the architecture of the great Pyramid of Cheops. And then you found you'd made a terrible mistake. One minute it was so thrilling: you were a sensitive, a child of the foreworld, sunk in a misty Gaelic dream; the next, you were in the grip of something elemental, malign. It was evil and it took you seriously, even though you were modern and smart as paint and knew about the Queen of Sceptres, the Horseman of Cups. There were things far more ancient than ghosts; spells that outlasted time. It was a chase and, without meaning to, you'd turned into evil's quarry. You stuck your pins into your little clay dolly and hated, hated. And all the time evil came closer — to you.

8

When Lou had lived in the sandhills, there'd been a time when she went to school. It was like Hell, walking each day down the town's neat streets, past proper people's houses with slippery red verandahs and the pebble-dash like little sharp teeth. In winter it wasn't so bad. Drizzles suited her; dwarfed by a lowering sky, a cold wind whipping your cheeks and no one in sight, you were brave. But in summer your shadow stepped forward to give you away. The flap marked LETTERS was Brassoed to a blinding perfection; there was always a hose coiled tight like a sleeping snake. Even though it was early, there were shivers of heat in the air. Lou longed to be in one of those gardens — lying lost under the walnut tree in shade. But the proper people ignored her approach. Those hedges were there to keep the likes of you out.

Lou was a Mundy. She was in the same camp as Mad Bob who fell off the telegraph pole and would stay an infant for life; as Wriggle, who was half Abo and would show you his thing for a penny; as all those barefoot others whose sandwiches were only beetroot . . . and they ate the bogies out of their noses, and it was good when Teacher gave them the stick. They weren't fit for Australia, being poor and common as dirt. Mother said Keep away. Though it was all right to give Wriggle a regular bashing — the filthy pervert.

And Lou Mundy was just as bad. Worse even, for with her shapeless dresses and downcast eyes she had you fooled she was convent-bound. The minx had this give-away hair, though — gold, almost to her waist. Who did she think she was? She had the cheek to dream — her, whose mother would do it with anyone.

Their eyes were constantly watching; whispered hate words pursued her down the streets. She went past the church, and its spire reached God in the sky, but he wasn't on the look-out for her. One day by the newsagent's it was all about Ella on the footpath, and Lou was sweating, she wanted to cry — walking into school on Monday was awful, for over the weekend you forgot the sniggers, the judging eyes. Your father deserted you by dying; the chalk marks said your mother was a whore. What does it mean? you asked Ella, and she hit your face.

Dreaming was Lou's only escape. It was a habit that softened the fact that she stood by herself at recess, and watched from under the pepper tree when it was hoppy or skippy or hidey. In the classroom she dreamed herself away from common denominators and history-book dates. Hard facts were Lou's enemies: she shrugged them off, and banished Teacher's droning voice. Till the cruel stick came down on her shoulders and she had to go out the front. Where, staring at the ceiling, she'd start off on dreaming again. Doing that, it didn't matter that she never got an invite to parties; that she wasn't friends with Dymphna Trott, prettiest girl in the school, who had the mulberry tree in her garden from which the chosen were allowed leaves for their silkworms.

She wasn't Lou Mundy at all, but had been kidnapped as a child, maybe from one of the summer visitors who came for the marine curiosities, and stayed at the temperance hotel. It was true, Lou was sure. She didn't belong with the people about her. She might be anyone; anything could happen.

There was an assistant in a West End hairdresser's, and a baronet took her to dine and she ended up stripped of her clothes and tied to a tree and coated with boot polish. There was another girl in a Sheffield razor blade factory who received an offer of marriage from an American business magnate, president of a corporation. (He saw her photo in an advertising circular. He sent it back with a ring marked round her, and wrote inside the ring: "May I marry you?")

The newspaper gave you hope for each day. Lifelong cripples were cured by prayer and cast aside surgical boots. Palmolive soap made you flushed, radiant, alluring. Mussolini's clarion cry was "Live dangerously"; Melba had promised Marconi to cooee round the world by wireless.

And there was Queen Maud of Norway. And Queen Ena of Spain. And the Infantas Beatrice and Christine . . . Thinking of them with their crowns and castles made Lou feel safe. It didn't matter that they were up the top of the world, and she was down the bottom. The kings and queens, the princesses and princes (even naughty Carol who had amours), did for Lou's saints. The wind kept blowing, sand was all over the verandah, but she went on believing.

And like a half-forgotten poem at the back of her

mind was Ella's past: drowned violets, a pair of goose-girl plaits floating after dead animals down a creek.

Dreaming sweetened Lou's life, but it wasn't something she could rely on. Most days that walk into town was real enough; you couldn't imagine away the woman Ella was now. On bad days, reality had power to shrink even royalty to human size. The Infantas bled every month, too; Prince Carol was a man with a doodle. On a bad day Lou's dreaming had the sense to turn modest: a sure escape-route meant relying on Alfred and Vi.

And then Ella died and Lou left the house by the lagoon. But she went to meet the new life with Tom beside her; and, from the Bon Marché's window, the bright lights of Adelaide burned dim. But Fish's treacherous hands drove them into the Hills. Where nightmare faded. Auntie lived at Sorrento and she let them past the front door: Lou had got in at last.

Auntie and her house were symbols. Doll, with her pale mouth and old-fashioned clothes was unquestionably respectable (it didn't matter about being an artist, when your pictures always came out genteel); she did for all those other proper ladies who'd snubbed Lou through the years. And Sorrento, with its fretwork trim and down to earth paradise garden was just the thing, too. The town near the sandhills had been full of houses like that.

The grandeur of The Frangipani Gardens wouldn't have suited Auntie, but it was perfect as a setting for Girlie. Who wasn't royalty, but had played a part in Lou's imaginings, too. Unbelievably, Fern Gully had introduced her. In the Hills, Girlie had got free of her society page image to reveal herself as perfectly mortal.

Those shaming schooldays had finally gained their reward. Somehow, all through them, Lou had kept dreaming. Against the odds, she'd believed and had hoodwinked her life into changing. The dreams were silly and sentimental, yet they'd had the potency of martyrs' prayers. It was as if, by the intensity of her feeling and her longing to get away, she'd willed Girlie to come.

Then, capriciously, Lou's dreaming took a false turning. At the Fig Leaf Ball, she'd probably danced Girlie out of her life.

And he was merely Pierrot — he was no one: she didn't know his name. His cheek had felt soft but he was a larrikin; it was disgusting, Girlie had said.

Lou supposed their friendship was over, but the very next day Girlie called. She was sweeter than ever; when they walked together, they linked arms.

Pearl was banished from Girlie's room, and it was Lou who helped her dress for an outing. And she did manicures; she held up the mirror so Girlie might inspect the back of her shingle.

Whenever Lou thought of Girlie — then and after — she thought of a flower. Her dance frocks had daffodil skirts, and she had a collection of artificial shoulder posies, and her clothes smelled nice because of the potpourri sachets placed among them.

But Girlie wasn't rose or bluebell. She resembled something hothouse; something strongly-scented with a sweetness that suggested decay. She was an exotic wax-like party flower — something white, with a hint of blush or bruise. Lou thought of spider lilies and magnolias; of the frangipani trees that clustered about the house, their clumsy branches spiked with pale blossoms like stars.

Girlie took Lou to the Arcadia Café's sixteenth birthday celebrations, and it was St Valentine's Day, so a little girl came on as Cupid and shot an arrow into the iced

91

cake on the directors' table. It was a whopper — three-tiered, adorned with sugar hearts. Everyone received a piece, and the orchestra played "Indian Love Call".

They went to the *New Ideas Revue,* and the Garden Theatre was *al fresco* and the fairy-lights in the trees lent an Oriental touch. The velvet curtains swished apart to reveal Mr Billy Maloney with his infectious humour and exaggerated walk. He twirled his silver stick, presented by his admirers in Brisbane, and sang "Princess Betty's Lullaby", his latest hit.

Girlie gave Lou status; through her, more dreaming would come true. For the *Renown* had sailed over the international date line — Monday becoming Tuesday on the stroke of eight bells — to reach Fiji. Soon the Duke and Duchess would be in Adelaide. Already the conundrum of the hour for many was whether they'd be invited to the Lord Mayor's Ball to be held in Their Royal Highnesses' honour. Lou longed to be included on the guest list. Girlie smiled sweetly, and said anything might be arranged.

Lou liked Girlie. But sometimes a small fear nagged. It was nothing — it was a warning. For Girlie was dangerous, part of Lou knew. But, knowing, part of her felt not fearful but excited.

She kept visiting The Frangipani Gardens; it had become more home than Sorrento. The O'Briens were so friendly, Lou felt one of the family. Even Pearl seemed pleased to see her. She started on a hymn as Lou went up the stairs.

And this day Pearl's voice was triumphant. She sang "The Lamb shall ev-er, ev-er reign". Lou wondered if Girlie would be going out, and what dress she'd wear.

But Girlie only wore water-snake shoes. She'd left off

her camiknickers, she sat at her dressing table naked. Up top she was more like a boy.

Girlie was combing her hair. She teased it out, till it rayed about her head in savage tufts. Then swiftly, brutally, she flicked them away. Now her head was glossy and smooth.

But there was nothing to fear. They were merely girls together. It didn't signify anything — the shiver creeping over Lou's body. They were girl friends . . . Girlie was skinny. Except for the silky private hairs she might have been a child. Looking at her, Lou felt bigger and clumsier than ever. Yet she felt soft, sort of floaty.

Slowly, deliberately, Girlie dabbed scent between her breasts. Nothing would be nicer than feeling her sharp-edged body press against you. Bruising, hurting. Now she was stepping into one of her beaded dance frocks. She was sheathed with jets and bugles. She glittered and rattled when she moved.

And then it was like playing at Ella, or standing in for Girlie's dead mama. Lou was holding Girlie; she was crooning nonsense words, whispering pet names.

Girlie was small and lost, and Lou must comfort her. But all the time the beads on Girlie's dress pressed into her skin. It was a torment. The beads were shiny black ants eating Lou's body. Girlie was hard and unmoving. Lou wanted to call out "Oh please". It was Lou's body that needed the comfort — she would let Girlie do anything. The voice was moaning, now, because little insects were marching over Lou, she would be eaten alive. And then the moon shone cold in her eyes and Ella's shadow went past and Pearl's voice screamed louder that there was light on the gloomy hills and the nations should rejoice, rejoice . . .

Did it happen? Girlie wore her silk kimono; they

were sitting side by side on the sofa, and she was pouring out tea. She smiled at Lou, and said it must have been the walk up in the sun that had done it. Lou felt dizzy. Everything was scary; she didn't want Girlie to leave her, ever. Anything could creep up and get you. Secret holes were bitten in the peach leaves; the baby oranges fell off. Aunt Doll stamped on snails and squashed caterpillars between her fingers. Fish's hand fluttered palely like a fan. Lou knew she was meant to tell Girlie something: she started to tell about Fish.

Lou loved Girlie. She was it and a bit, and Lou had a pash. She was gone on Girlie and she wanted to giggle and rub up against her. At school, girls had crushes on Dymphna Trott. You wheedled her autograph and wore a bangle engraved with twin hearts. Lou had felt scornful, but now she was enslaved, herself. She was telling it all — about the hairs up his nose and what a reader he was and how he'd caught her in the schoolgirl corset.

Girlie laughed his fingers away. He was only a man, he was nothing. Men were the giddy limit; they were something like monkeys. "Oh, my dear," said Girlie, and she moved closer on the sofa; she started confiding, and the world went drab and dark. What had been written up in the lavatory at school was true. Man and woman love was a small thing — comical, worthless.

Lou sipped her tea and shuddered. Without meaning to, she thought of Ella. Even she had taken men seriously.

9

It was perfect weather for rambling about the Gully. The sky was a soft blue, the sun was gentle. Peaches fell into the grass with muffled thuds; the apples grew ruddier each day.

Tom and Charlie were two friends walking past stately drives lined with agapanthus, cottages buried in hydrangeas; strawberry gardens and beehives . . . and then you turned a corner and it was like entering a different country. There were melancholy crags and glens that would have suited robber barons; there were groves of inky pine trees and, behind everything, the gum trees rose distantly in tiers. They looked unreal, infuriating. So softly scalloped, so regular . . . a few pale trunks wavered stilly, pretending to support that great flocky mass. They were nothing like trees should be . . . more like a dream landscape of moss.

Almost every day, now, they were together. While Lou made for the model nursery, Tom dodged traps and trenches and tunnelled towards Charlie's hut.

Though the wild bees were always on guard he was

never stung. Caesar jumped up in welcome — he seemed Tom's dog as much as Charlie's.

And they walked past neat rows of cabbages, signs saying CHERRIES FOR SALE; walked among blue-green paspallum grass and: "Apple of Sodom . . . scarlet pimpernel . . ." murmured Charlie, and everywhere Tom looked there were flowers: spider orchids and the brown and yellow ones — bunnies or donkeys they were called; and wild pea and something pink and twining like fingers . . . It was so pleasant. Tom broke open a peach and it was yellowy inside, juicy. Juice trickled down his arm as he bit into it, and Charlie spoke of interesting things.

Most people seemed to walk about dead. It was as if some ague crept upon them early on, so that by the time they were adult, they were embalmed. It was nothing physical, though — no, the mischief was mental. Proper people were deadly. Their minds were stiff and unyielding; all the magic images of the earth were captured inside them, and every scrap of freshness got pondered away.

But Charlie's mind had stayed alive. It was up there under his battered hat, darting about, acknowledging the wonder of summer verging on autumn. Walking with him, the natural world wasn't diminished.

And Charlie told stories of hobgoblins, satyrs, and dragons; and there was a man who went out with a burden and he tumbled in the slough and Mr Worldly Wiseman dwelt in the town of Carnal Policy . . . it sounded a good book, and Tom was allowed a lend. And gossamer spiders wove balloons to sail through the air; the trap-door spider had a nest lined with silk. In the sea were sponges called Neptune's cup and Venus's flower basket; in the sky was Vega in Lyra and Arcturus in Bootes.

And certain plants, roots and barks possessed medicinal properties. You drank the juice of herbs and your sickness abated; you rubbed on marshmallow ointment and the sore on your lip healed up. Charlie knew of fever powders and sweating teas and itch salves; decline syrups and strengthening cordials. He taught Tom the names of plants and their uses. This was tremble blossom that removed the yellow tinge from the skin; that, tansy, the flowers of which, dried and powdered fine, might be taken in treacle as a sure remedy for worms.

Charlie was a herb doctor. He traded his tinctures and ointments for a basket of hens' eggs, a pot of jam (Caesar had been payment for a speedy cure in a bad case of scald head). The people who consulted him were old-fashioned; the modern world appeared to have passed them by.

When Charlie had been a young man, he'd walked through the Hills with an old lady called Lizzie Potter, who'd taught him the things he told Tom. Lizzie had been noble and benevolent, a skilled doctoress in roots and herbs, but because her clothes were eccentric, and she kept to herself, the proper Gully people scorned her. It was curious to think that her tin house had stood where Sorrento did, now; that, all those years ago, Charlie had gone behind the squeaker hedge to visit her.

Charlie stooped, and knapweed was hard to pull, so he cut at it with his knife. He would mix it with sugar and boil it up. The infusion would be drunk for pains in the bones — yes, knapweed had been put in the world for use in curing. But some plants were malevolent; you mustn't touch them. Bindweed, that twisted in intestinal fashion, was known as the devil's guts; enchanter's nightshade, with its dusky flowers, induced delirium and death.

Sometimes when they walked about the Gully they found things even more unwelcome. There was another clay manikin in the creek; HAZEL was written on a piece of paper nailed to a tree. Charlie crumpled the paper and sighed. Someone had believed that Hazel, whoever she was, would decline as the paper was destroyed by wind and weather.

Their walk would be ruined by a find like that. But when they reached the hut it didn't take Tom long to cheer up. There was the Nondescript and the Mermaid to admire, and then they'd drink tea and Charlie would tell about his travels.

For, once upon a time, Charlie had travelled the world with a dwarf and an albino in a one-horse caravan. "Hi! Hi! Hi! Walk in ladies and gents. No deception, no 'umbug about this show!" cried a man standing on a tub by the side of a flaming gas jet . . . Charlie told the story so well that Tom felt he was there. He saw the fair ground's striped booths. The roundabout gallopers raced on, and he queued to see the Human Frog who could eat sponge cake at the bottom of the aquarium without also swallowing water.

Charlie had known exotic cities which no longer existed. St Petersburg in January had only five hours of daylight and the coachmen were wrapped in newspaper under their great-coats. There were Caucasians in astrakhan hats with silver daggers stuck in their belts. The troika drivers wore peacock feathers in their caps . . .

It was a fairy-tale told to a child. They were equals, but part of Tom was still a little boy. He never knew what Charlie was travelling for; what he had to do with a dwarf and an albino.

The part of Tom that Charlie seemed to consider

most valuable, most grown up, was the part that others despised. Once Tom had asked him if he could brew up a remedy for his fits. Charlie had shaken his head. Tom's fits, he said, weren't the sort you dosed with anti-spasmodic tincture. Tom's fits were a special gift, he should treat them as something precious.

But Tom hadn't had a fit for a long time. Instead, he'd started having curious dreams.

Charlie was always in them, but strangely altered. In the dreams he'd turned into Cockroach. Dreaming, Tom was pursued by a mumbling horror with tangled elf-locks and fingernails like spears. But the glass eye was worse, because it had come alive: in the dream it was swimming in blood.

When he reached the hut next day, he steeled himself — and it was all right: the eye was glassy and dead. But Tom wondered about the scar down Charlie's cheek. A voice whispered treacherously inside his mind that Charlie's past must indeed be villainous.

And there was a dream that featured Charlie doing his cures. But he was muddled with Peg Fox. It was Peg who'd killed Ella; there'd been blood then, too. It was Peg's voice that came from Charlie's mouth and told about the child like a walking skeleton with his head wagging backwards and forwards. A clock pendulum head meant water on the brain; meant catnip, rosemary, red sage, marjoram, wood betony and pennyroyal, but Peg's voice didn't agree. Charlie's mouth opened and Peg recommended henbane that was Satan's eye and snapdragon that was his beard and garlic that flourished wherever his left foot touched earth outside the Garden of Eden.

But night was a thing that passed. Daytime always replaced it, and Tom went on loving Charlie. Though the dreams grew worse, and the Judas voice kept up its chat.

For Charlie *had* to be a villain. Even if you disregarded the scar, there were other pointers to go by. Why was it that he hid away his hut, why did he seek to avoid most other people? For, sometimes when they were walking, Charlie ceased being Tom's wise friend. He skipped off the road to become elusive, vanishing. It was as if the leaves or the grass had signalled a warning. Tom stood unaccompanied on the Gully Road as the person — it might be the butcher, the postmistress, anyone at all — approached. And if Charlie didn't go to earth, but stayed his ground, Tom felt even more alone. For, unaccountably, Charlie became a stranger, a mere parody of himself. He was almost Cockroach, as he scowled ferociously, as he muttered vindictively at the unlucky passer-by.

It was as if Charlie had an enemy that had charmed its way into Tom's head. It hid somewhere near his ear; it whispered and whispered, determined to persuade him to deny his friend. But Tom's love was too strong for the intruder to wear away. He stopped his ear against the insidious voice, he cast Peg and her devil plants from his mind. Nothing would separate him from Charlie.

In the end, it was Aunt Doll who did it. One afternoon she was waiting for him when he returned to Sorrento. She'd stopped being calm — her face was swollen with crying, her eyes were full of pain. She knew where he'd been. An anonymous letter had come, telling of Tom's friendship with the Gully hermit. And it was wrong — now Auntie's voice duplicated the one that maligned Charlie in Tom's head; now he heard them speaking together. Cockroach was dangerous. He stole away little boys and put them in a stew-pot to simmer; he sliced them up fine to eat for his tea.

But Auntie didn't say that. She was shaking her head, her mouth was woeful. She was saying that she had never asked for the responsibility. Other boys went to school and why not Tom? Oh dear, oh what should she do?

Then, like an answer, Lou appeared. Tom ran to meet her. She had saved him from Alfred and Vi; he knew she would defend him now.

But Lou wasn't alone. She was accompanied by her friend, Miss O'Brien. Tom didn't trust Girlie. He scowled as she ruffled his hair, as she playfully pinched his ear.

Auntie went on with her lamenting. Tom listened with interest. There was this boy, and he'd grow up a savage. The letter reckoned he was bad enough as it was, being strange and abnormal, lacking a fixed place in the scheme of things. A regular boy cared for marbles and Meccano, but not this one. Aunt Doll should be ashamed that he did nothing but read, or stare at the sky, or go walking with a dirty old man.

Lou didn't say anything, it was Girlie who spoke. "Don't fret, Miss Strawbridge," she said, "I've thought of the very thing."

Tom could go up to The Frangipani Gardens and Girlie would give him lessons — Girlie doted on little boys. And there was Granma, who'd relate Irish history; and Boy, who was a hero, to provide a manly example . . . and Brother Wells, who was always popping in, would delight to have a go at Tom, too.

10

The frangipani trees clustered about the house. It was the Hills, where you built your summer residence to escape the city's heat, but they were here — jungle trees, trunks twining, boughs branching in clumsy lattice. Strange branches, grotesque. Blunt fingers, marked with notches like mouths. But it was only where the old leaves had been. The branches kept growing, the leaves were always at their tips. The old ones, left behind, turned crinkled — they were banana-blotched with brown, then they fell off. The new leaves were a fresh bright green. They were green fish, wagging stiffly about the flowers. Frangipani: five petals of creamy white, deepening to yellow in the centre. Tight-clustered, with a wedding-day smell.

It was a scent you put on your hanky — it was hair oil sticky, sickly. And the flowers were so fleshy, but the branches were so dead (they were like reindeer antlers decked with posies); and if you reached up and broke off a leaf, the tree bled milk. It was horrid. The milky tree-blood was all over Tom's fingers. He rubbed his hand on his shirt, but the stickiness wouldn't come off. And there were so many of them. Twining together, blocking out Granpa's house. They were monsters that flourished on the frosts and temperate summers that should have killed them.

But Girlie wiped his hands on her hanky, and led him further down the garden. And here was the yucca that was Adam's needle with its waxy bells and bayonet leaves. And bird of paradise, hibiscus, gardenia — and in Tahiti, Girlie said, gardenia grew out on the coral reef. Tom couldn't help it: he liked her. She held his hand and it was Granpa's house not hers, but she made him laugh. Cherry pie, she said. And: Jockey's cap lily, baboon flower. The datura's dangling blooms were angels' trumpets; cassia was scrambled eggs.

She knew as much as Charlie; she wasn't Tom's enemy at all. They were children together — brother and sister, laughing at the grown-up world. If it were learning, Tom wouldn't mind school. The sacred lily of Egypt poked up pink from the pond; the American tulip tree was sixty feet high.

But Girlie was little. She smiled at him and Tom grew taller and saw she was minute. It was curious, but for a moment he felt like someone else. Tom was another boy and he looked at Girlie and wondered if she might be blown away like a Father Christmas thistle by the wind. She was small enough to fit in the horse's ear, the snail's shell.

Tom was charmed by Girlie. He sat down at the drawing room table and crossed his ankles and she told him a tale about proper boys.

It was school, and there was no end of larks and holly leaves in your pillowcase and an apple pie bed. And you said Friends, Romans, countrymen and had midnight feasts with pork pie and oranges, sausage rolls, raspberry three-corners, shrimps, ginger beer, sardines and she would go on with the story tomorrow, about what happened when the house master surprised them in the dorm. But now Tom must start on his learning, and each day it was the same — the walk in the enchanted garden holding her hand, and another chapter of *The Boys of Barminster*, and then Tom learned that the rainbow wasn't God's promise, but just the sun's level rays shining past you towards a cloud. And the stars were huge boiling suns; there was no man in the moon — not even a lady. "The moon is a dead world . . . The sun is composed of fiery gasses."

Rapidly, Tom slid into Girlie's power. He was as much hers, now, as Lou.

Tom's encyclopedia stayed shut because its pages were only good for a laugh. How could he have believed its nonsense about the lark's song of hope at heaven's gate, the nightingale's magic trill that has thrilled poet, prince and peasant in all ages?

Birds formed Class Two of the vertebrates. They ranked next in importance to mammals and were warm-blooded, with both skeleton and backbone.

He wasn't the same boy. He begged pardon and never picked his nose. Girlie combed his hair back and said a gentleman didn't smile too wide.

And their young came out of an egg. They had horn-covered beaks instead of teeth, and a special apparatus called a gizzard. And they sang when their voice muscles were rocked to and fro by air — but Tom didn't hear them.

He was walking through the orchard, and there was a bird on every twig. They watched him with round staring eyes. But no song, not a sound, came from their beaks. Something was wrong. Only his feet seemed to know what to do, as they tramped through the grass. And then he looked up — he didn't know why. And they were over his head: they might be the geese that used to come to the lagoon. Flying across the sky, making alphabet letters. He came alive again. He clapped his hands at the unlikely overhead wonder. And then the birds on the apple trees moved their ruffled throats and sound came pouring out.

When he reached the model nursery, when she held his hand and led him about the garden, the exotics had lost their appeal. He wanted those drab bushes that looked like weeds, and Charlie's cloak moving amongst them, its folds full of their smell. And the bees would be round the big gum tree. They had a nest there, and in time Charlie would put the honeycomb in a chaff bag and hang it over a kerosene tin. The honey would drip-drip down . . . Charlie might get almost a tinful.

Girlie shook him. Cow's udder plant, she said and he was meant to laugh. Poison lily, she said and her voice was bitter. He was himself again. That was Ella's rustic bridge . . . the house had belonged to Granpa.

They went inside, and he slouched in his chair and scowled. She closed the textbook and introduced some people.

They were a rum lot, the O'Briens. Besides Girlie there were three others. Mister was a mechanical doll who never stopped grinning; Boy was a smooth-faced dandy; Granma was a painted ancient confined to a chair.

Only they weren't like that at all. Charlie had spoken of seeing with magic spectacles — Tom felt that he had them on, now, as he looked at them one by one.

Mr O'Brien wasn't just a Molly of a man. Buried

inside his weak-hearted body was a fiend who yearned to escape. Sometimes, for an instant, the captive fought free, and a hateful look overwhelmed the old man's placid eyes, the smile was struck off his mouth. The red in his face worsened to an alarming shade of lobster, he flexed his great helpless hands. Then, a tremor crept over him; he clutched his heart as if it was worn to a silken thread, and the stranger disappeared from his eyes.

And Boy wasn't handsome as a filmstar. That perfect complexion masked a hopeless condition. Behind it, the boy-hero was a monster with a skin that resembled flaky pie crust. His face was cauliflower-pitted, and by his temple was a mortal wound. It was deep enough for your thumb to fit in; it throbbed and ached ceaselessly. Under his smooth-skin disguise, Boy O'Brien was a walking deadman, he should wear a tinkling leper's bell. The war had done unspeakable things to him. Ypres and Bullecourt were terrible names.

And Granma wasn't crippled, but — still talking — rose light-legged from her chair and did a scoot with you across the world. She pushed back generations till it seemed like the Middle Ages, and Tom was in a charnel house where the bodies were the colour of blackberries and so swollen the coffin lids wouldn't fit.

Gran was a cranky horror. Tom had to sit in her room and even the pot plants could scare you. There was crown of thorns; also blood-leaf plant and tear-drops. But Gran didn't cry as she drilled you in history. She was jolly as a sandboy as she related Ireland's woes. Now she was up to the convict ships, which meant traversing the deep under bayonet point to be shot out like rubbish on a bare foreign strand.

But Tom couldn't take any more. He screamed, till

Girlie came in and said she would teach him. The snake lady helped her, and they twisted his arm, and put him in a room, so dim. And Ireland was the Niobe of the nations and Tom was a doomed felon and on the mantel, on either side of the remember-me pansies, was a man. "My darling Jim" it said underneath, and to the left he was ordinary in a Sunday suit; to the right they'd made him a soldier.

This man was dead, Tom knew, and the door was locked and he'd never get out. The room smelled of pimple cream and the chamber pot under the bed; and there was a little animal, scurrying madly. But no, it was Tom's heart — jumping with fear. He was alone, so afraid. Girlie turned the key and said he would learn. She hated him, and Tom crouched low and wasn't sure who he was. For, again, he felt just like this other boy (Girlie had hated him, too). Seeds were rattling in Tom's head, there was a hairy caterpillar crawling close. There didn't seem any hope (this other boy had been scared so badly that he'd given up feeling), and then it was worse, for the soldier in the photo stepped out of the frame, he jumped off the mantelpiece and came towards Tom on the floor. Tom tried to hide, but the soldier wouldn't let him — and then his face went different: then it wasn't Jim, but Charlie.

The room stopped being haunted, he was no longer afraid. He moved about calmly, inspecting Pearl's things. The Bible on her bedside table was open at the worst bits in Revelations. Beside it was a pin-cushion, with the pins pricked in to spell TOM.

But their evil couldn't hurt him. Though Charlie was no longer visible, Tom sensed he was still there, guiding him, keeping him safe.

When Girlie opened the door, she smirked over her

shoulder at Pearl. It had worked, she said. The little beast was tamed, he'd cause them no more trouble. Really, it had been too easy — Girlie sounded almost regretful as she pushed him from the room.

He was clever, he had them fooled. His real self was something like an earthworm, coiled deep in his decoying body. No one could get at him, no one even knew worm was there. Tom was wily. At Sorrento, at The Frangipani Gardens, he took the rôle of docile zany. It was simple to do — merely a case of smiling smarmy and wearing a soft expression in the eyes. Yes, Tom's eyes were jelly-soft, so agreeing, as he pretended to be hooked on their baited words. It was easy, easy. Your head kept nid-nodding and after a while they believed in their robot creation. Fancy — such success, by just sticking in pins. Even Gran gave up trying to scare him. There was no joy in relating horror stories when you couldn't count on reaction.

They believed in their model waxwork boy, while the old Tom kept safe. He was still the misfit who picked his nose and rolled it, and had fits and heard birds. Tom stayed uncouth and ignorant, even as he sat with fingernails picked clean, feigning interest in the lying textbooks. All the time he was out of their reach. He went barefoot and threw himself down in tickling grass and chewed at the soursob's tart stem.

He was back on the cliffs. He walked past the shelter shed with its stale stink of urine; seagulls keened and it was good — so blue and gold — with the sun the poet's orb, and the shot-silk waves. The jetty stalked forward on damp criss-cross legs, the fishermen were statues along its rail . . .

Perhaps it was Charlie who helped Tom escape through his thoughts. Since that spell in Pearl's room, the hermit was constantly with him. Their friendship was comforting . . . the marbled waves wallowed in, satiny, and curled and dashed and leapt at the cliff. Spray broke in icicles and waterfalls, and then the sea drew back with a hiss. And the sky went lilac, cold crept up on the air, the thorn bushes shivered — but Tom stayed cosy, he felt he was hugged by Charlie's cloak . . .

It was something he didn't understand, and he was glad. For knowledge only took you so far, and some sort of knowing held you back. The textbooks told you all, they told you nothing. Charlie was nowhere near — it was a fact.

Because Tom was such a lackbrain, they thought it safe to let him stray from the house. They put Granma in her Bath-chair, and it was his task to push her round the Gully. He didn't mind. Now she kept quiet about famine and disaster, he bore her a grudging respect. She was wicked and so ancient she ought to be dead, yet she still got a kick out of life. Part of her stayed young and oddly innocent. She took Tom so much for granted, that she'd started confiding her secrets. The curls were a wig (beneath them, Gran was as bald as an egg); she liked pineapple pattern better than star pattern in crochet; she kept well, she would live for ever, because she sucked on a barley-sugar lolly when she woke in the night.

Tricking them was child's play — Tom felt almost sorry for Girlie as his simpleton pose took her in (it was too easy: Tom was too clever).

Then one day when he and Gran were setting out, Girlie drew him aside. How would he like to attend Fern

109

Gully College and be made into a proper Catholic boy? It was a school of growing consequence. The Archbishop came for speech night, there was a resident Monsignor.

And Tom's real self laughed himself sick at the idea, but *their* Tom — false Tom (who was so convincing you'd think he was true) — thought it over as he pushed the Bath-chair. How there'd be the apple pie beds and soapsuds in place of whipped cream . . . and braided blazers, straw boaters, midnight feasts (*The Boys of Barminster* had featured such things).

But it was a laugh, of course, and Charlie was nudging Tom's mind. Saying *Careful*. Saying *What about the birds and being free?* Tom didn't want to end up caught and tame — did he?

Suddenly Tom felt a terrible anger. Why wouldn't Charlie let him alone? He only wanted to be ordinary; he was tired of magic and nightmare.

11

Once he'd been Tom who lived by the sea; he'd had fits and counted birds as his friends. Those days were over. He'd chosen to become a boy who was going to school to learn a love for the Mass and the Sacraments, a devotion to Our Lady and the Rosary.

But, the decision made and the day set for Girlie to take him to town to be measured for his grey serge suit, Tom wasn't happy. The more everyone said how lucky he was, the worse he felt. For Charlie had deserted him. Tom thought wistfully of the perfect days they'd spent together — their walks through the orchards . . . the Nondescript, the wild bees. But those days were part of a past that was done with; Tom had lost the knack of vivid recall that had hustled them forward to be part of time present. He could no longer escape through his mind; he was alone, now — Charlie was nowhere near.

He couldn't depend on Lou, either. Though she often walked beside him while he pushed the Bath-chair, she seemed far away.

She was there the day the College crocodile came

into sight. Tom guided the chair to the side of the road, and Gran crossed herself as a Brother went past.

There were two sorts. One lot was pale, with flower-stem necks and silky beards; they were Christian Brothers from the Spanish Inquisition, with John the Baptist eyes. Frankincense and myrrh floated about them in musky cloudlets; there was a constant jingle from their rosaries (they were the Lord's annointed, for sure). You knew they had scourge marks on their backs, and could bear Chinese burns and scissors grip in wrest-ling. But they were so pale, so silky and scuttling, that they didn't seem like men at all; they were more like those soft grey scurrying things you surprised under stones in the garden. And the other lot was Irish, with washerwomen mothers. They relished taties and bacon rind and sang "The Dear Little Shamrock"; they had dented red faces, wax in their ear-holes, steel-rimmed specs, clumsy boots. And you knew they sweated as their money-box mouths groaned prayers (but they never saw visions), and cracked a joke as they raised the stick to swish you. They coached cricket and footy but missed out on a fresh-air odour. What teased your nose wasn't exactly B.O. — it was a queer smell (fusty, fur-tive), as if, because there wasn't a lady about, they'd been wearing the same singlet for months. Brother Keogh was an Irish one with that sort of smell. Brother Wells didn't fit in either camp.

His nickname was Swells, because he was such a swell in his dress. If he hadn't been a Brother, he would have worn Oxford bags and swagger shoes. As it was, he had scent on his hanky, and Tom thought him rather a duffer (though Swells was kind enough, having lent Tom a copy of Bishop Gilmour's *Bible History* that told of Heresies and Rome Destroyed). Lou didn't appear to like him much, either. She drew back behind the Bath-chair, she looked the other way, as the crocodile edged on and brought Swells closer.

And these boys were Roman Catholics. Holy medals hung from their lapels. But they had pimples and boils just like everyone else.

Then Brother Wells had reached them, and for an instant the crocodile divided. One part kept moving forward, the other paused. Swells smiled at Tom, and said how nice it would be to have him at school. And it was flattering to be stared at by so many eyes — Tom felt important, he felt guilty for having judged Swells harshly. Though there was a queer hollow look about the Brother's eyes (it gave him a hungry look) and, even as he spoke kindly to Tom, he spanked a small boy's head.

Then the crocodile was one again; Brother Wells moved away, and the seniors were a disappointment. Most of them were weak specimens, lanky and pale, with blood as thin as an old wife's third cuppa.

Only in the very last row was there a group who seemed up to scratch. There were four of them: they had swagger and down at heel boots. They kept laughing and digging each other in the ribs; one of them aimed a spit bomb at Swells's back.

The spitter was a capital fellow, a picture of bright sauciness and beaming mischief. His eyes were round and blue; his nose was a miniature dumpling. His blond hair curled over his forehead like the ruffled plumes of a cockatoo.

And the funny thing was, that the blond boy was staring at him — or so Tom thought at first. Then he realized that the look went past him, and knew it was meant for Lou.

And now the boy had fallen out of line. None of the

Brothers noticed. The crocodile kept advancing, till it rounded a bend in the road.

But the boy was left behind, and Lou had stepped forward to meet him. Gran cackled sourly about young love from her chair. Her old eyes were greedy, they ruined something beautiful.

He was a country boy, but the country he came from was different to Lou's. Instead of a lagoon there were ranges, though you couldn't compare them to the Hills. Up north, there were no hedges of monthly roses, no Sunday School picnic bosky dells. His ranges were savage; they sprang at the sky like arrested waves, for ever on the verge of breaking. They were ancient and fissured, wrinkled and whorled; their colour was what you noticed most. In summer the dominant shade was camel's hump dun; autumn and winter lent traces of green; spring meant the reds and purples of wild hops and Salvation Jane.

Summer was the season Garnet liked best. He used to sit on the verandah and stare at the changing sky and listen to the faint screech of the windmill and see — but not see — the stark corrugations of the iron shed beside it, and the dusty road. There was a pepper tree, too, and — behind everything — the shaggy pelt of the rise. You had to strain your eyes to catch it — that fiddly pattern of porcupine-grass, that constant wag and quiver.

The windmill sometimes fell silent, as if stunned by the heat. Sometimes he'd go round the back, step into the wiry sea of weed and walk to the cemetery. It was quicker to take the road, but he liked coming upon it through the grasses.

There were rusted tin leaves and china roses; several stunted trees, a few humped bushes. There was a clump of aloes by the explorer's grave. There were stars of lichen and:

> Death little warning to me gave,
> But quickly called me to my grave;
> Oh, haste to Christ, make no delay,
> For no one knows his dying day.

And it was true, for Minnie his mother was there. Pretty Minnie Lloyd, who liked new dresses and had chosen the fanciful "Garnet". She'd hated the town; hated the flies and the grasshoppers that threw themselves into the hot wind. She'd sat on the verandah, flapping the palm-leaf fan. He put his head in her lap and the moon was a nugget of gold, tipping the earth.

In the cemetery, too, were lizards and bull-ants and gleaming pieces of quartz. And the explorer had seen the British flag placed in the centre of Australia, he'd tramped to the shores of the Indian Ocean, then come here to die. The headstone mentioned pluck and endurance and loyalty, and Mother repeated the words softly. Garnet must never forget the explorer's example. He must become a man she might be proud of.

At evening the sky was mild. It looked the way you were taught to paint it in water-colour — pale and watery blue in the dip of the hills, merging to darker blue above. Then it changed to a pearly mauve; then everything was bathed with amber light. The ranges turned velvety, the earth was pink, and galahs flew over his head.

It was cooler at dusk — the terrible oven heat had crept away. But stones still felt warm under your hand: the warmth of the day had sunk into them . . .

It was a mining town and Dad had come to make his fortune. To begin with, there were boarding-houses and a butcher, a baker, a pub and a general store. It couldn't match the copper mania of last century's sixties, but there was a feeling of prosperity and gladness. The place was alive with the hum of machinery, the sounds of hammers and drills. Donkey teams carried the ore to the rail-head where it went on to the port. There were bullock teams, too; sometimes ore from mines further north was brought down on camel-back by turbaned Afghans.

Garnet was born in the house built of native pine. Minnie was happy enough at first. She tended the little garden walled with corrugated iron. There was a grape-vine and a fig tree and an oleander. The verandah roof was supported by saplings, grass came up between the slates of the kitchen floor, but she sang as she polished the shiny black stove and coaxed the ivy geraniums to grow.

The geraniums flourished, they screened the veran-dah with a leafy curtain, but it was water that beat them in the end. The ore was still coming out, but they had to put in bigger pumps. What with the cost of pumping added to that of everything else, it wasn't worth it. There were plenty of mines closer in, untroubled by water, that could sell at half the cost.

People just drifted away. They pulled most of the mine buildings down and sold off the machinery. The shaft caved in; only the slag heap was left.

A few stayed on. The police sergeant who'd worn a coat with silver buttons, even on the hottest day, took it off and turned into a lay-about in a singlet who swore there was gold in the creek. And there was a Chinese gardener who grew vegetables there, too — he mostly

116

worked at night, carting buckets of water, crooning to keep evil spirits away. But even he gave up over summer. Then, each day was a scorcher, a regular brick-fielder, and Minnie used to swat at flies and cry. Maybe she went a bit mad — she dragged about in her petticoat and Dad grumbled that the place was a pig-sty, and the kid's howling would drive him bananas. Yes, Dad went mad, too — the ranges had got him. He wouldn't leave: he was waiting for the mining revival. And he joined forces with the policeman, he raved about seams of gold. He went down to the creek each day with his pan, and dredged up a phial of gold specks. But he had sense enough to take over the store; he went in every week to the town near the railway and came back with provisions in the buggy. He scratched a living of sorts. He had his regulars, and wanderers were always passing through, and they started up a sanatorium for consumptives, and there were always artists come to set up their easels in spring.

Life wasn't too bad. Dad drank, but the empty bottles caught your eye — upended, stuck in the earth as an edging to the geraniums. Minnie pulled herself together when summer was over. She'd pin on her cameo and walk with Garnet to the explorer's grave, and there'd be fuchsia streaks in the sky, and though she had wrinkles and rough hands she reckoned it had been worth it — for Minnie was a Catholic: marrying Dad had been a sin.

Sometimes she went to the city to see her family. Garnet went once, too. It was so dreary it seemed like Sunday, with a smell of moth balls and a carpet patterned with swirling leaves. Minnie had all these brothers and sisters — Garnet had all these uncles and aunts. And the Madonna on the wall stepped off a cloud, and they clicked their tongues because he didn't go to

Mass. They wheeled in a tea-trolley with a squeak, but the cake had little seeds that stuck in his teeth and his cup made a terrible wobble in its saucer and he slopped tea and knew they saw. They were tutting and staring with quizzing-glass eyes, and there was a cocky that shouted *Cocky got a cold* and *Where's Minnie?* And they said didn't he take after his father; they said he was a regular Lloyd.

But some of them came up after she died. They cleared their throats and made their offer. It was their duty, they said; Minnie would have wished it. His father nodded his head: he turned into a Yes-man who gave Garnet away.

And they said God took special care of the mother-less, that a day would come when He would wipe away all tears. And they sent him to Fern Gully College and at holidays there was the house full of relatives with look-alike faces. Someone had been to Egypt, and there was a collection of miniature mummies in the drawing room. Also crazy-work vases and a clock trapped inside a glass dome. Its tick was melancholy, muffled, and Cocky still cried *Where's Minnie?* and Garnet hated his life. But it was easiest to keep smiling, to play joker in the pack. On the surface he was carefree and smiling; inwardly he longed for his past.

Yet Minnie faded paler and paler. He forgot the crinkly lines round her eyes and the summer sweat beads along her lip. He couldn't hear her voice any more; he didn't remember her smell. It was queer — he knew the sprigged pattern of her Sunday dress by heart, but he couldn't recall her at all.

But Dad stayed a real man. He had a prickly face and a crease between his eyes, and when he came back from the pub his breath was innocent, it smelled like scented cachous. He had stains in the armpits of his work shirts, and that last day he'd sat on the verandah with his traitor's head bowed, and the leaves of the pepper tree were silver in the sun — they tossed and shrugged, they waved and beckoned.

Garnet stayed homesick for his own country. He longed for a summer that would burn the fake gentility, the cheap politesse, away. He was tired of living cramped, he wanted to feel a big emotion. The country he'd left wouldn't leave him alone; nostalgia was at him all the time.

One day he'd set off, start walking and never look back. He'd be an explorer and find his father and the ranges again. The hot wind would blow off any last trace of city smallness. He'd sleep beneath a curdled navy sky, speared with the Southern Cross; wake when the first touch of yellow crept into the day and the flies started on their daft tizzy. Everything would be there, just the same: skeleton bushes, spiked and needled and pinned; spinning slats of the windmill, dusty road. The range rising up like a flat cardboard cut-out; the roots of fallen trees stretching skyward like stranded meteors.

He told Lou some of it, and she, in turn, told of Ella and coming with Tom to Aunt Doll. In some ways, their lives were similar. They both had dead mothers; they'd both been torn from their beginnings. (He assumed Ella to have been as virtuous as Minnie; he took it for granted that Lou yearned for the lagoon.)

But Garnet was going back. His father was waiting, with welcoming arms stretched wide. He'd saved for years to give his lad an education, even though he

119

lamented daily they were far apart. He was a pillar of the community, splendid in his male pride; once he'd been an explorer. Garnet's dad had been misled by mirages; he'd done battle with crocodiles and furtive blacks, eaten kangaroo mice and drunk the queer fluid that flowed from the bottle tree . . . and in the end he'd got there: he'd marched doggedly to the centre of the continent and planted the Union Jack . . . Yes, Garnet was lucky, he had a hero father and "Mother" meant not flesh and blood but a gentle ghost.

He was a romantic, who carried a withered rose in his pocket because it had been worn in Lou's hair. He sighed and said he'd thought of her consantly since that waltz at the Fig Leaf Ball. He'd dressed up as Pierrot for a prank, yet it wasn't merely the sheer devilry of breaking bounds, of escaping Our Lady and Our Lord and all the other holy monsters, that had led him there. More than anything, he'd been propelled to the Palais by fate — without doubt, they'd been destined to meet. As soon as he'd seen her, he'd known they were perfectly suited. And they danced and it was bliss, but Brother Wells was a masquerader, too, and his eyes were suspicious, and the car was starting back for the Hills, so Pierrot had to slip away . . . He looked at Lou with moony eyes and swore he'd known he'd find her again.

But he was male, which was something disgusting. You should fasten the window, stuff the chimney, cover up the keyhole so one didn't get in.

(Lou had been learning a lesson. Girlie had taught her well.)

She tried to hate him, but she couldn't. Indeed, listening to his moonshine proved a tonic: Lou was strengthened enough to shake off the phantoms that kept plaguing her head. She let him take her hand and they left the road and sat in someone's orchard. Apples had fallen in the grass, the sun poured down, and about them was a smell of ripeness.

Nothing made sense, but Lou didn't care. For so long she'd felt herself the dupe of some novel conjurer's trick. Her head had been mazed with hateful whispers; she'd imagined that inside her dwelt another person — a stranger who'd claimed her mind. It was like being joined to an evil twin, who smiled and sneered, even as you felt like weeping. The simplest things had appeared complex; corruption was everywhere.

And now, in the orchard, everything changed. He said they would always be together. For no good reason she believed him.

12

The Duke and Duchess were in New Zealand, now, seeing hot springs and boiling mud. The Prince of Wales Feathers geyser was specially soaped for the occasion; school children did poi dances and grouped to form the White Rose of York. The Duke had donned mufti for the tour, and showed a preference for splendidly-cut tweeds and a felt hat with the brim turned down. There was crowd hysteria in Christchurch and an epidemic of fainting fits in Dunedin. Some people waved the stars and stripes because the Dominion's stock of Union Jacks had been exhausted.

And in Sydney the landing stage at Farm Cove was being decorated with flags and streamers, palm trees and plants; while in Adelaide finishing touches were being given to a red gum casket, embellished with carvings of eucalyptus leaves and wattle, which would contain the city's loyal address.

They were nearly here — but Lou didn't feel much interest. Without meaning to, she'd stopped caring about royalty. She felt the same about filmstars. John

Barrymore was coming to West's as Don Juan, but she didn't give it a thought.

Every day Lou met Garnet at the back of the College. It was their secret place. You crossed a plank bridge, and by the creek were lemon trees tangled in creeper. She waited amongst stinkweed and fennel till he came running down the slope. The trees seemed to crouch and twist; Jap ivy had turned them into a series of leafy chambers. He spread out his blazer for her to sit on. They were alone with shimmering green shadow play all round them, and the rush of the creek so near. He picked flowers and threaded them in her hair. Frogs made a creaking noise; midges rose in dotted clouds.

Nothing could hurt them, not even Girlie. Lou hadn't been to see her since she'd met him. It was Tom Mundy who went up through the orchard each day, now.

Lou stopped thinking of Garnet to worry over Tom's set face and miserable eyes. He'd nodded mechanically when she asked if he really wanted to start at the College.

Then, one morning, instead of Tom going to the model nursery, Girlie came to Sorrento. She had a dead fox round her neck and a velours vagabond hat on her head. "My dear, how I've missed you," she said and her sweet voice was steely (how could Lou have ever thought she'd escape?). Girlie wondered if she'd forgotten that it was today they'd arranged to take Tom to Adelaide to be outfitted for school.

He looked so lost standing beside her — he was only eight years old. Lou couldn't let him go off with Girlie alone. She pulled on her coat and followed them down the path.

The Dodge was outside the gate. Boy would drive them in, Girlie explained to Aunt Doll, and they'd come back on the afternoon charabanc. It would be dark by the time they returned to the Gully. Would she be agreeable to Tom and Lou staying at The Frangipani Gardens overnight?

Lou sat close to Tom in the back of the car and the old bewildered feeling crept upon her. The Hills had ceased being friendly; she couldn't remember Garnet's face. A change had come and, though the grass was still green and the leaves of the apple trees were a goldeny-bronze, all the colour seemed drained from the day. Winter had slunk up unseasonably like a cunning grey wolf. The greyness had got into everything. The sky was a dirty white; the landscape was tinged with gloom. The cottage gardens they passed looked merely pathetic, part of a flimsy toy world. The Hills were famous as South Australia's best bit of England, the Tourist Bureau ran a bus through daily, but the camellias and azaleas, the hawthorns and birches, didn't add up to much. They were swamped by the menace of an ancient sombre world. The gum trees pressed forward, and Girlie and Boy, Lou and Tom — they were toys, too, as the tourer skidded, then rounded another hairpin bend towards Adelaide.

Only Girlie was spunky enough to stand up to the day. Her scent smelled spicy; her mouth was a shiny gash. She was gay, and so supremely confident.

And now they were in the city, but Boy didn't drop them in Rundle Street, which meant all the big shops. Girlie smiled into her foxy collar, her eyes sparkled from under her vagabond brim, as she told him which way to go. It was a surprise, she said, a special treat, but they only ended up in the parklands.

Boy drove away and Girlie led them towards an artistic fence. Part of the parklands was enclosed, and you paid your money to the man in uniform and he let you through the gate. There were Jap bamboos in tubs, but where were they? It was a compact spot with plenty of room for the glass cases in their wooden frames. The demonstration enclosure occupied a central position and — like the cases — was quite escape-proof.

It was the Snake Park, and you looked through wire netting and the snake trainer stepped forward in high-heeled boots. All round him were his charges — python and rattler and tiger; whip and carpet and diamond. For a moment everything was still: you shuddered, for danger waited, poised. The adder raised its head to strike, the cobra writhed closer. The rattlesnakes, instead of hissing, coiled tight about an awful sound. It was dry and cold; it sounded faster and faster.

But he had a nice smile and a toothbrush moustache: he would win through. He was Mr French, the curator — a cultured gentleman, lately arrived from Capetown, and snakecraft had always been his hobby. There was nothing sinister, nothing to fear. The wire netting was close-mesh; pot plants made the cages homey, and a printed card listed their occupants' names. The snakes would help in Adelaide's fight against vermin; already, five hundred rats and mice had been devoured.

Girlie listened, entranced, while Mr French explained that there was no danger, really. The snakes treated him like a tree, a mere place of abode. "You see," he said, "I always touch the snake before I pick him up. That is to let him know that it is I who am near." Even the more savage specimens appeared to know their keeper. He felt sure that — in some instinctive fashion — they realized he loved them.

The taxi back to town took them past Rundle Street again. After a while things began to be familiar. It was

Hyde Park Road; it wasn't a surprise when they drew up outside the Bon Marché.

The drapery's shattered plate glass had been replaced; the shop windows featured everything correct and most favoured in smart wear for the coming royal functions. There were georgettes powdered with sequins, tulles encrusted with crystals; feather fans and half-moon shawls.

No one could mistake Girlie O'Brien. Alfred came rushing over from the cash desk at her entrance. When he saw who was with her, his smirk faltered. But he recovered to play big bro' to perfection, as he crushed Lou to his pin-stripes and playfully punched Tom in the chest. How could they have done it? he cried — how creep away to the Hills without a word of farewell? Till Doll's letter had come, Vi had been anguished; horrid fears had flooded her mind. There was always a larrikin type out waiting to molest you.

Vi still seemed to think they'd had lucky escapes (though not from the Bon Marché). When Alfred ushered them into the drawing room she was startled enough to switch off the serial story. She had to be helped to the sofa, their reappearance gave her such a turn. When Girlie explained they'd come to purchase Tom's suit for school, Alfred escorted him off to Men's Wear. Vi recovered a bit then.

Because of Girlie, it was best cups for morning tea, and Vi cocked her little finger and talked as if she had marbles in her mouth. "We had lovely times together, didn't we, Louise?" she said wistfully. " . . . *Didn't we, dear?*" she said threateningly, when Lou didn't reply.

Adolescence was a trying time, and families should stick together — not that Vi wasn't sure Lou and Tom were perfectly happy with Auntie. Ah yes, the world was a terrible place . . . Vi took a jammy bite of sponge sandwich and reflected happily that kiddies didn't seem to smile any more, and the Government kept letting in foreigners, and the Duchess hadn't included a single black dress in her wardrobe. There were all these men walking round Adelaide who didn't wear hats, and in Bucharest King Ferdinand was dying, and in America the suicide epidemic among students raged on (the latest had done it with iodine after amateur theatricals in the school auditorium, where he'd received great applause).

But Girlie said she had a tragedy to tell that would easily better that. What did Vi think of dirty old men? What if there was this girl, an innocent, and she was in your care, and this creature touched her with his monster hands?

Then Girlie and Vi were talking low; then Vi winced and suggested Lou should take a look round downstairs.

The wooden balls of the cash railway trundled backwards and forwards. The bad penny was still nailed up by the cash till as an awful warning; the shop girls still had their shingles. There were some lovely lines in tabby silks . . . here was the Bon Ton and the Royal Worcester.

Fish had the same nostrils, the same celluloid collar. They'd sack him, of course.

She dodged behind longcloth nightgowns; he pinned her by stockinette bloomers. "Pretty pussy," he crooned, and he winked as if they were old friends. It was queer — she didn't hate him. Girlie had got him, too.

His mouth was watery, it had an eager look. He was rubbing his hand against his leg. "Naughty girl," he said, baby-voiced. "I been so lonely without you." And where did she go, what did she get up to? Did she let fellows monkey or treat her to intoxicants? Fish was holding the front of his pants, now, he was bobbing down as if he was in pain. "The hot blood which courses through the veins of youth is stimulant enough," he said. His voice sounded like a groan.

And another good Bon Marché line was Australian emblems. You could sew them to cushion covers, table centres, runners. You chose from rosella, magpie, emu, kanga . . . Lou was safe, for Tom was beside her. And Girlie and Vi had come into the shop, and Alfred was with them.

Fish's face was tender, his eyes were dreamy. He was a gentleman-assistant with revers to his waistcoat and a tape measure round his neck. He had scented hair and fastidious grooming, and tonight, after washing his smalls, he'd tuck himself in early with *Dr Ricordi's Interesting Book for Men*. Life was good. He smiled as he moved forward importantly in answer to Alfred's summons.

Lou had a new dress and fairy-tales were true. For the looking glass reflected a princess and it was a dress that shone like the sun and came out of a nut shell. Nonsense. It was white tulle, and came from one of the big shops. It was perfect. There should be turtle doves and three drops of blood falling from a pricked finger on to snow. It clung up top and there was a little floating cape edged with crystal beads and beneath it her arms were bare and, despite the cape, did she show too much arm, too much chest? But Girlie said thinking like that was suburban. "We'll take it," she told the shop lady and opened her purse.

How kind Girlie had been. After leaving the Bon Marché, they'd lunched at the Arcadia, then gone on to more shopping. Now, back at The Frangipani Gardens, Lou anticipated the Lord Mayor's Ball and dressed up in Girlie's presents.

She had all-silk stockings and satin slippers, and she sat at the dressing table and shut her eyes while Girlie did things to her face. There was powder on a swansdown puff and scent from a bottle with a stopper like Napoleon's hat. It was lovely sitting there, submissive to Girlie's soft fingers. Lou felt lazy, she felt shivery with pleasure. Now Girlie was combing her hair; she was coaxing, teasing, making waterfall waves and ringlets.

It was a fairy-tale, a dream, and to suit it there must be candles instead of gas light. Lou looked in the mirror and Girlie held the candlesticks high, and there were stars glimmering in the glass — one of them was caught in Lou's hair.

And Girlie glittered like an idol in gold-sequinned lace; Tom wore his new suit; Boy and Mr O'Brien had carnations in the lapels of their dinner jackets. For the evening was a celebration (though Girlie didn't let on for what): Lou was allowed a cocktail.

By candle light the dining room was transformed. The crimson wallpaper and curtains had turned exotic; the sideboard was alive with mahogany gleams; even the catch-crumb drugget seemed a thing of mystery. But the table was best of all. Its ice-smooth damask surface was set with sparkling crystal and silver; its centrepiece was a trumpet-shaped vase of frosted glass. At its base were piled peaches and grapes; above them, was a mass of frangipani.

And the candles had pink silk shades, the napkins

were folded into water lilies. There were chocolates in silver shell-dishes and it was a game — working out what to do with the knives, forks and spoons. And there were so many glasses: a wine glass for each sort of wine that was served. Tom stuck to lemonade, and Boy raised his eyebrows, but Girlie insisted — so soup meant sherry and first entrée, champagne ... by the time Lou reached dessert it was sherry again.

Then they were somewhere else, drinking coffee, and the liqueurs stood ready on a tray. Lou's head felt fuzzy, and there was moss over the floor, and a new friend sitting opposite — oh, she was pretty with wedding flowers in her hair. But it was Lou in the looking glass; it was the drawing room carpet, and Girlie had tucked the frangipani behind her ear. It smelled so sweet and oh, Lou felt dizzy, perhaps she was even tipsy, for she felt so happy and she started to laugh. For how comic it was: Tom and Lou, visitors in Granpa Strawbridge's drawing room, despite having Ella for a mother. If only Tom wasn't such a spoilsport. Why did he ruin it? — sitting on Granpa's over-stuffed ottoman, with a miserable expression on his face.

Then Tom rose, he left the room, and Lou forgot him. Probably he was going up to bed.

It was what he meant to do — climb the stairs to Granma O'Brien's room where he was to spend the night on her couch. He couldn't bear to stay in the drawing room. Their voices grew louder, until they seemed to be screaming, and Lou sat among them, as pink and white and innocent as the Christmas tree fairy, with her big arms bare and her hair as yellow as straw. She was a doll, with her silken legs sprawled wide and her dress ridden up to show her garters. She was shameless, but at the same time so innocent.

130

The door shut off the brightness; he groped his way towards the nigger-boy newel posts, and then the Christian Brother's hand gripped his wrist.

Tom could have escaped. He'd been strong enough to leave the drawing room — even Mr O'Brien's devilish eyes and Boy's leper face and Girlie's savage mouth hadn't been able to stop him (though perhaps they hadn't wished to). But in the hall he turned weak. It was a worse sort of danger; it was evil compounded (and now Swells's hand was trembling as it fondled his cheek), and Tom was two boys: and false Tom was strong, while real Tom was weak. It was false Tom — so passive, so perfectly obliging — who let Swells lead him into the kitchen.

Nothing could happen. The hand that led him had manicured fingernails, but it belonged to someone under holy orders. No, nothing would happen to Tom.

Yes, evil was all about him and he liked it. Real Tom saw — he cried a warning. But false Tom, so perfectly childish, walked blithely on.

Saucepan stand and mincing machine were instruments of torture; Cook's big knife had a dangerous edge. And the kitchen table was just as sinister, for it was strewn with the things from dinner and the shining plates were dirty and the wonderful fish in its mayonnaise blanket had dwindled to a skeleton backbone, the turkey with its frilled-paper legs was plundered as bad. The sherry-tasting trifle was reduced to a smear of whipped cream; the maid who'd served like an angel was snoring, with dribbles down her muslin apron.

Then the kitchen lamp was a false moon bobbing over Tom's head. It lit their way, but it made the dark about them seem blacker, and the antler branches of the frangipani trees look bigger, blunter than ever. For they were out in the garden, now. The stars were cold and uncaring as Brother Wells led Tom across the gravel. Under the tulip tree they went, past the humped shapes of exotics, till they came to a house of glass.

And they walked in a wonderland where the plants of all climes and seasons bloomed together. Everything was marvellously muddled — the lamp showed you bits at a time. The glass walls were latticed with ivy; veiled with filmy sprays of fern. Doors kept opening and closing, for the model nursery's greenhouses were linked. Now they walked through one where the flowers — hyacinths, cyclamen, lilies of the valley — represented every gradation of white. Then they were moving through a jungle. Instead of cloying bridal-wreath scents, there was the damp smell of moss. Slimy green stems were everywhere, there was a sound of running water. Tom had chosen to come here, he held Brother Wells's hand, but he felt abandoned, afraid. The oil lamp left blackness behind them, and how did you know the glass house you'd left still existed, that you weren't cut off for ever from an everyday world?

Past the next door it was a jungle world, still, but the familiar oiled-silk greenness, verging on black, was alive with rainbow colours. The lurching stems, the jagged leaves were starred and splintered with flowers. They were immaculately frilled, sticky-stalked; hung with fronded fringes and hairy dingle-danglers. Their petals were shiny as enamel, waxily opaque . . . some seemed freckled with gold dust, others appeared specked with brilliants.

Tom walked through the orchid house and it was all right at first. It was so kind of Brother Wells to share the perfect place with him. There were orchids like butter-flies, some were even comical (this one had a cockatoo profile, here was a parrot's beak). There were snakes' tongues and rats' tails — but was it so funny any more, was Brother Wells so kind? Tom shivered, he couldn't help it. For it seemed the most frightening place in the world. Now he was surrounded by glistening eyes as bad as Mr O'Brien's; by a host of pouting lips as treacherous as Girlie's.

Tom was captive, and the Christian Brother's fingers were claws. They dug into the earth that anchored those glossy stems, to reveal a foul mass of roots. And some orchids had tubers that clustered in fingerlike lobes. They were black as sin, they signified Black Mary's hand, and that tuber, chopped small and mixed with wine, made an amorous cup that was as good as nasturtium leaves for turning girls frisky. Brother Wells wouldn't stop telling these things. Tom didn't want to hear. Orchids didn't mean just dogs' stones and bulls' bags . . . not merely Black Mary or the devil's hoof. They were only plants — so many anthers and pistils, sepals and petals; remarkable for brilliancy of colour and grotesqueness of form. But Tom was caged by glass and outside was the night and the orchid eyes quizzed him, their bee-stung lips would gobble him up. Yes, orchids were eyes and lips; were daggers and spikes, spurs and clubs.

Yet he was merely Swells, who'd lent Tom the book that told of the promise of the Holy Ghost and the temporal power of the Popes. But Swells's legs were moving strangely under his skirt; under the black skirt his legs rubbed together as if they were itchy. And now Swells's legs pressed against Tom and his body bent over him, his great face leered close. He was hideous, with his dog lips the colour of strawberries, and his cheeks flushed as if they were rouged. But he was

Brother Wells who should be sitting safe at Fern Gully College on a fat chair of buttoned morocco, his white hands turning the pages of *Pictorial Lives of the Saints.* But his hands were on Tom. He was a Christian Brother, but he spoke harshly, yearningly, and shut his eyes.

Tom felt a thrill of horror — he was Daniel and the lion would devour him. But he felt excited, too; he longed for the awful thing to happen. But Swells's body pressed closer, Tom would be suffocated . . . Suddenly he was so frightened that he felt his identity slip away. Even false Tom disappeared. Tom was no one, now; he was helpless. He was just a threatened child — any child at all, in the grasp of evil.

. . . but some tubers were called Christ's hand. Charlie used them in a nerve tonic. The tincture smelled unpleasant, but when you held the bottle to the light it glowed a beautiful crimson.

Tom was saved, for suddenly Charlie's voice was in his head, cancelling the evil out.

He was himself again. He bit at Swells's hand, he kicked at his ankles, and then he was free. The orchids tried to catch him, but he hit at them, too. Glossy petals fluttered about him as he made his escape. The Christian Brother cursed and limped forward with the oil lamp, as Tom darted into the garden.

13

Lou lay on Girlie's bed, but really she lay by the sea.
She was back in the sandhills; she was dressed like a
bride, and the glittering scarf of water lurched forward
to break in shivering pieces on the rocks, to curdle spent
on the sand. They were two bodies twined together with
bridal creeper — Lou's big body and Girlie's small one.
Now Lou's body was jellyfish soft; now it was hard as
coral, and Girlie's fingers felt all over it, they were
explorers finding secret places. Lou kept her eyes shut
and saw the sea come scalloping in. She used to walk
among the soursobs on the cliffs. Out on the reef foam
dashed at the sky, as the sea cast up its shells, its fringed
weed.

Girlie's nimble fingers practised sleight of hand; they
were clever and made rippling waves, they tangled in
tickling seaweed — it was strange, so pleasant: Lou lay
in Girlie's arms in her new tulle dress, and the skirt
would be crushed, but she didn't care. She was drunk,
she was spelled. Girlie had done wonders with animal
mesmerism, aided by champagne and sherry.

And at Fern Gully College, Garnet was dreaming. Lou and he were lost in the ranges. The sun beat down; they were perplexed and misled by mirages. Lou couldn't keep going much longer. Her face was haggard, her person emaciated, her spirits wholly sunk . . . And in the studio beside the quince tree, Doll was taken with a sudden attack of the shivers, and "Evening Stillness" went wrong — she couldn't get the tender gum saplings right. Her paint brush went trembly; goosie walked over her grave. She knew she was meant to make a start on a different picture . . . And out of the simmering cauldron came a pungent smell of spearmint. It wouldn't be long to winter, so Charlie was brewing cough syrup. He stirred and stirred and then he had to stop. For the child had need of his mind again — he was out of the orchid house, up with the old lady, but evil was still about. Caesar knew, too. The hair had risen on his back, a snarl started in his throat . . .

And at The Frangipani Gardens, Eily Casey sat up in bed. She'd taken the wig off and her head shone bald through the baby fluff; her hands were liver-spotted, she had a cataract in one eye, her hearing was nearly gone. But it was still she — still Eily, though they called her Gran, though when she looked in the mirror she saw a face like a fig and there was a spit bowl and a chamber pot beside the bed. But a barley-sugar lolly did wonders: Eily won through. It wasn't age that had got her, but the Irish phantoms. They wouldn't leave her alone — she couldn't do without them.

And Tom wasn't ready for sleep. He didn't want to undress before her perving old eyes — that was one thing. Another was a worry that kept nagging his mind: *Where was Lou?* Gran was on again — about corpses and coffins and empty gruel spoons, but the words were mechanical, they didn't count. When the change came, he was as much taken by surprise as she. For, suddenly, feeling got into her voice. It stopped being Gran's voice, old; it was Eily's voice, young.

"Lord Jesus, save us," she cried. "The fallen angels have come." They were laughing like geese; their boots were too big for their feet and were clapping, clapping on the roof. Didn't Tom hear them, too?

It was a sound like thunder. It was a sound in the air like an army marching. The drums were beating, and now they were overhead.

"Lord save us," Eily cried again. She crossed herself, she was shivering. It meant someone was going to die. It was a punishment, there was evil in the house.

It was the fighting at the hour of death. The friends and enemies of the dying among the dead were fighting to claim . . . but whom? Was it *him* or *her*? But Girlie's papa (who was Eily's son) — his heart had let him down already; already, for years, he'd been one of the living dead. Poor soul. For, of course it was him they'd come for — and it was a blessing, too. Eily had nothing to fear. She was fit as a fiddle and her bowels kept open, she wore a scapular round her neck. But she wished she had a sprinkle of holy water; she wished Girlie had never been born.

And the four winds of heaven blew upon the house, and a storm came carrying ruin. Birds started falling from the sky — pheasants, partridges, pigeons. And rooks fell, too. And rabbits, hares, even cats . . . Tom was having a fit, it was thrilling. It hadn't happened for a long time, and this time he stayed awake and watched it happen.

He was screaming and thrashing about. He ripped at the suit that had him neatly marked off as a Catholic; he threw pot plants. And then he wasn't just Tom. It was a fit with a difference for, as well as watching himself have it, he felt he shared it with another boy, too. Tom joined forces with that boy who'd been scared by Gran and hated by Girlie all those years. They were together; they were one, as they pulled down Jesus from His hook on the wall and kicked at His swooning face. There was a wonderful shattering of glass as they took their revenge on the events of that terrible day and night, and of all those terrible years. For it was Jesus they kicked at — it was snakes and Vi, orchids and Swells; and Mama's dying, Papa's indifference, Girlie's hate, Pearl's sinuous embrace.

And Lou heard him. He was walking proof of Ella's misdeeds; because of him, she could never pretend away her past. All her life she'd been answering those screams; she couldn't ignore them now. His voice broke through the poetic sea sounds. Tom was having a fit and he needed her. She pushed off Girlie's arms; she slid from the bed.

And all the time the drums kept sounding, and Granma wailed of famine and pestilence — of feasting on nettle-tops, wild mustard and watercress; of the assuaging of hunger with seaweed, which too often meant the acceleration of death. And, saying it, she fell back on the pillow and Eily got free. Granma O'Brien was dead.

And it was a fairy-tale, but Girlie had changed rôles. Without warning she was the spiteful queen who held out the poisoned apple. And Snow White took a bite and was put in a coffin of glass. The birds of the air bemoaned her.

But, instead of owls and ravens, it was Tom. His voice keened on, calling her to him, and Girlie said: "If you go we're finished. If you choose the brat you'll regret it for ever."

The new dress was crumpled; the frangipani flowers were crushed. Though they smelled stronger than ever. They were wedding flowers, graveyard flowers.

But Girlie was so small on the bed; she was such a tiny thing. Lou's will faltered. Girlie's head was bowed, she was crying.

. . . and perhaps they might still be friends . . . and perhaps the hedgehog would like to be petted, but its quills would prevent its being pleasant to stroke.

Girlie was unapproachable. She was hedged with hate.

The little person on the bed raised her head and Lou saw a stranger. She was a little wizened lady with a painted face, but the paint was smudged, all the colours had run and she was crying, but she was smiling, too — it looked like an exercise for sagging muscles.

Lou said her name. "Girlie," she said. But the face was a mask and its eyes spilled tears and its mouth didn't answer. This mouth was stretched wide. It was a try at a smile, but there were no laugh lines at its corners . . .

And, to begin with, it was dark; Tom was feeling his way and he was frightened, for he heard a voice calling. *Lou, Lou* it called and it was a voice he knew — it was his voice, Tom's, but each time he heard it he got a surprise.

He watched it happen from a great distance. The child stumbling in the dark, the voice calling on. And how there started to be lights; how servants appeared in shawls and curl papers, and there was the snake lady in a dismal nightgown and the old man clutching his heart and Boy, immaculately braided and frogged. And they were crying *Who?*, *What?* and the child was clever. His mouth kept shut, he made himself invisible as the mouse in the wainscot. He crouched, he hid, and their footsteps went by him, the lights passed above his head. Lamps and candles and matches wove patterns up and down the stairs, then the gas brackets came to life with a hiss and he wasn't so safe. But they had found her, then; they didn't give Tom a thought . . .

Tom's voice was close, now. Lou opened the door and a gust of wind blew in at the window. A storm raged about the house.

And he ran into her arms — he had found her. They were brother and sister and they stood together, and no one would tear them apart.

But Granma O'Brien was dead and fierce squalls passed over Fern Gully; there was thunder and lightning in the sky.

Lou felt clear headed, but tired. How could she have forgotten Garnet and their innocent love? She held Tom's hand tighter. If they could reach Sorrento they'd be safe. But Girlie came towards them, showing her teeth. It was a smile of hate, and Lou couldn't move. Though she clung to Garnet with her mind, and she thought of Auntie, too. For surely Doll was the best possible antidote to evil. She was so smally respectable, so dull. Robur tea — grown, dried and picked under the supervision of white men — was her favourite drink. She wore spun silk vests and mercerized lisle hose.

And Tom shielded his eyes, for suddenly a dense cloud of birds flew at his face. Their wings caused a considerable rush of air; they sang and sang, making a continuous clatter and noise. And then the birds were gone; then a snake coiled round his arm, and though he shook it off it fastened to him again . . .

But it was a dream, everything was but a dream, as Girlie screamed that Lou was a slut. Girlie had seen her lying with her pretty boy under the lemon trees, and Lou was a cheat who would live to regret it, And, as for Cockroach — he would suffer, too, and how had he got that scar, why did his hands like to linger on Tom? And Doll Strawbridge — well, Lou could stop pinning her hopes on to her, for she was a worse whore than even Lou's mum. Ah yes, why not ask Doll to open that locked door in her studio? Lou would find out the truth about Auntie then.

And hailstones as big as teacups fell on the Gully, a giant's fist kept punching the sky. Fiery whips lashed the moon and the stars shook with fright and lumps of ice were embedded in melons. Roofs were dented as by hammers; pigs were killed outright and horses and cattle severely bruised. It was a night to remember, and Lou and Tom were out in it, battling their way to Sorrento.

Apples skidded under their feet, and the orchard dipped till the moon was tangled in a thorn bush and a net of branches snared the stars. But then they were climbing up again — the moon floated free, the stars lobbed back into place. Every step you took made the world different. After a while the last hailstone fell.

In the Hills you trusted your neighbour and didn't bolt your back door. They crept up the passage like thieves. At last they were safe in their room.

Tom was asleep in a trice, but Lou lay awake. She couldn't stop remembering Girlie's words about Doll. They were lies, of course. Auntie was perfectly respectable, the very opposite of Ella, and: "Only odds and ends from Flower Hill," she'd said (meaning chipped potichomanie vases, *The Veiled Bride* in Parian ware), when Lou had asked what the locked door in the studio led to.

But why should you lock up trifles? — it wasn't idle curiosity that kept the question teasing Lou's mind. She longed to forget Girlie and her maligning voice; longed to trust in the virtue of Auntie's maidenly stockings and vests. But she couldn't. Until she saw for herself what was behind that door, Doll's reputation stayed challenged.

So she went out into the garden and down the crazy-paved path. She passed grapevine, nasturtiums, lavatory, and it felt like one of those nights when she'd explored the Bon Marché. She was Lou, escaped from them all — alone in the night, on a quest of her own. She felt strangely elated, wonderfully brave; she might have been a knight-errant, set out to defend Auntie's honour.

And she came to the quince tree and wondered at what she saw. For the studio was a place of mystery that exactly suited her mood. Its panes of glass defied the darkness and flamed with colour — ruby and amber and inky blue; even the glass that was no colour, shimmered with icy brilliance. For Auntie was a vestal virgin who'd gone off to bed and left her incandescent mantle lamp behind. It was like day in the studio, and first Lou inspected the half-done picture on the easel. It was as tame as ever. Quite lifeless, but ladylike, therefore reassuring. Though Doll's brushes had been flung down at random, they were caked with water-colour, and she hadn't bothered to screw on the tops of her paint tubes — this wasn't so propitious. Something seemed to have made her stop painting and leave the studio in haste.

142

Lou held the Aladdin lamp and faced the door in the corner. And it wasn't locked, but stood open. And Auntie had lied.

The room was full of people. Lou was surrounded, the figures pressed forward. The child stooped by the creek and violets swam into her hand; the young gentleman extended his fingers and assorted nosegays sprouted from their tips. And the foaming sea dashed in and a boy and girl were pecked at by birds; and here they were again, stepping from the belly of the big sleeping woman — the girl with a suitcase, the boy with a book. And there was a man from the Bible with a beard full of bees, and a lady with breasts like roses. She was shameless, splendid, with every part of her come alive. Tears trembled in her eyes, her rippling red hair tumbled loose in a shower of sparks, and she held out her naked arms and offered her milky body. The young man accepted, but his floral fingers were spurred with thorns. It was a punishment, she was ripped and bleeding, and the bearded prophet whirled his stick and the roses and violets, the anemones and lilies were slashed to shreds by his rage. He made a storm that tore at green jungles and the boy escaped, but the goose-girl was caught in a wedding-veil shroud and the glittering golden princess loved her as the serpent inched closer. But the girl managed to dodge; she held the boy's hand and the wind lashed them, poisoned apples rained down, as they ran through the orchard towards the house behind the hedge. It had only just happened, the paint was still wet.

The paint wriggled in anguish, sometimes it had been put on like worms; other times it lay thick as mud, and you saw the marks of her fingers — for a brush wouldn't do; she must mould it, caress it, bully the picture right.

143

In the studio her brush twanged coolly as she swilled it in water and the paint was diluted, muted; it went on the paper tasteful and pale. But in here she used canvas, and there were the worms and mud — the paint was different, it smelled excited. And the colours were vulgar; they didn't beg pardon as they assaulted your eyes. There were trees like green flames and blood-red seaweed and stars as yellow as butter. And all those people, acting out their secrets without shame, pushing into the open the unmentionable dreams.

The room was crowded with pictures. Auntie had been painting for years and dust fell on people Lou didn't know; and on a supplementary cast representing the trappings of high romance: passion flowers and love birds; tropical gardens and parrots and blue-faced baboons.

But she was old, she never got married; she was cast for a rôle as written off as any walled-in nun's. But Auntie hadn't played fair. For her prissy lips and Queen Mary dresses were part of a monstrous disguise. The paintings proved it. She wore her hanky up her sleeve and was always washing her hands and never once had she farted by mistake — but it was all a front for a passion worse than Ella's.

Part Three
Doll and Charlie

It was now — it was then: Flower Hill was home, not Sorrento. And, to begin with, Doll was content. She was Childie — the only one. She had a scalloped flannel petticoat and feather stitching on her collar and a red silk sash. She went for picnics in the trap, and the teapot kept warm as toast in a little padded basket, and you were allowed to hold the chicken legs in your fingers. Father took off his jacket, he rolled his sleeves, but Mother sat under her holland sunshade lined with green, so no ray of sunshine should touch her skin.

And the days made a pattern that turned into years. Now it was summer when you slept under only one sheet and prayed there wouldn't be a bushfire. Insects flew round the lamp and the passion vine was in fruit; then it started to be autumn and the leaves went the colour of boiled sweets — sulphur and pink and winey-purple. And there were poisonous berries, and fires that smelled of eucalyptus. Then winter: the wet hills looked varnished and there was frost on the lawn. Spring meant wattle with its sneezy smell — it was everywhere.

They were a family of three, and Doll sat at the table with the velvet cloth and drew quietly and with perseverance, as if nothing existed except Mother and Father and herself, pencil and paper.

She drew and drew, she always had. It was a gift, they said, and Father patted her head and called her the foreign name. *Wunderkind,* he said, and it wouldn't matter ever again that she couldn't think of words to say when visitors came; that her body went stiff and she felt strung together with wires. They stared at her, because Father was rich and proper and he shouldn't have a daughter like that. Her eyes felt weak, they kept blinking, and they lowered their voices — they said it was a pity about the spectacles. Her lips went so dry that her mouth disappeared, and they asked had pussy got her tongue (it was a joke, but Mother didn't laugh).

But Father had said his *Wunderkind.* He bought her a paint box and a sable brush you must lick to a point. And they walked hand in hand through the Hills and the road corkscrewed down to valleys of fruit trees and hard-hearted cabbages, ivory white parsnips, onions as big as cricket balls. Then Father put her on his shoulder and they went up-up-up to the summit, and Adelaide was a great city, it was Athens of the South, but Doll saw it shrunk small. Father's finger pointed out the Gulf, the Harbour, the Bay. Doll saw them all; she saw midget steamers gliding into port, trailing silver shivers behind them.

Well, if you didn't count Mother's snapping eyes, it was a perfect life. The visitors didn't often come. They were mostly three (you didn't count the servants, either), with Father a gentleman jingling money in his pocket, and afternoon tea on the lawn: quilted tea cosy, milk jug painted with violets; hedgehog cake, chocolate

148

iced, bristling with crushed walnuts and finely chopped dates.

But the older Doll got, the plainer she grew. Mother mourned the red hair and freckles; she had her banished from the nursery and chose another tot to take her place. Ella came and took everything. The rocking-horse and Bubbles, even Father. And now the drawings were ugly; they were wolf people Doll drew, with shiny snapping teeth and she felt dizzy when she did them, they were a surprise when her head came clear. Father wasn't much interested, but: "Why so ugly?" Mother cried. "Why can't you draw something pretty?" So Doll's pictures started to be careful — the teeth kept inside the mouths. But people could always be danger-ous; pimples and wrinkles crept in, and Mother cried "How dare you — that isn't my profile." So the people were buried in landscape, and Doll had instant success. She did the frangipani trees and the nymphea pond so well.

Mother was easy to hate. She gave whippings and scoldings and put you in the corner. It was she who made you lower your drawers and squat behind the arm-chair while she pushed up the dreadful hurting thing like a jelly bean because you couldn't do your business. You were unhappy. You would run away to the real Australia; eat damper and have black boys for friends.

But Doll was a young lady, now — she must put away childish thoughts. Life wasn't too bad. There was a laxa-tive you ate for constipation, now, and she went to the School of Design. She drew Greek gods and felt pity for Ella. For little sister had a worse affliction than art. She wasn't plain, she wasn't pretty and Mother didn't know what to do. For Ella was beautiful, she was the fairy-tale princess exactly, and Father loved her to distraction.

Mother couldn't bear it. She called it unnatural behind the locked door. Doll eavesdropped, it was a mystery she had to solve. She heard Mother's voice lashing his love to bits. Ella was punished, too. Mother cut off her hair.

And all these things were pictures that hid in Doll's head. She knew she'd never forget them, that when it was safe she'd let them out. She thought of the paintings she'd make; they'd be so exciting, and her life was so dead. Father ignored her, he was a frozen man with hungry eyes; Mother said "What will become of you?" But she drew, she had authors to read (an author whose works you were fond of seemed like a friend). She was happy enough — she was utterly miserable and no one knew. Mother said it was a blessing the girl accepted her lack of looks.

But Doll saw herself as someone lovely. She loved her red hair — how it was frizzy and the scurf fell like pepper and salt; and she loved every freckle, and her eyes were blue marbles, their lashes were sandy spikes . . . But they called it being ugly, though she couldn't see it, herself, as she crocheted another doiley for her hope chest; as she went on blindly believing she'd marry, be artless and ordinary, against the odds.

Mother shook her head. Seventeen, and the girl abhorred parties and balls. She was without an atom of romance.

Yet Doll used to walk through the orchards. No one was about, it was solitary as Eden, with jungles of sweetbriar, meadows of snowdrops and jonquils. It was spring, and she lay in the grass and stared at the sky, and it stopped being Australia — it was England, anywhere, a country out of legend. And then she blushed, she didn't know what to do, for someone was watching her.

150

A gentlemanly young man had come to stay at Gladwish House. de Moles had lived there always, and Miss Diosma was the only one left. She was an invalid, a Christian lady, who did good deeds from her bed of pain. The young man was a distant relative from Home. A thorough Englishman — but delicate — he'd been sent to Miss de Mole for a rest cure. The Gully mamas peeped at him. He wore tan shoes like Lord Randolph Churchill, and a soft-fronted shirt. Also a scarf with flowing ends, and his hair was a trifle long. But he might be a Tennyson, a Paderewski — he was always reading a book. And Gladwish House guaranteed class and his accent was English, refined. There'd be cash, for sure, and the Gully mamas asked him to tea, but he was eccentric, he never went. Poor young man, perhaps he was shy. He just read his books; he was seen walking with old Lizzie Potter, who brewed up messes of herbs.

It was this young man who saw Doll, and started to be her friend. They met each day, and he admired her drawings and read her poems from a limp-covered book. He was so clever, but he had chosen her, and Doll's fingers held the pencil that shaded in apple trees, but her mind made a picture of a wedding. But then he saw Ella — she took him away as she'd taken Father from Mother. She was only a little girl but the man loved her so much he did magic, and in the end he outdid himself: one day he disappeared.

He was cured, the Gully said. He'd gone back to England, and the mamas sighed (what a catch he'd have been) as they started to forget him. Doll prayed she'd find him again, but Ella didn't give him a thought.

She was a child, but she was also a woman. Doll was all those years older, but she'd never be a woman like that. Ella could make you feel strange. She stared when she talked, as if the words had a secret meaning. Her skin was so white and soft you wanted to pinch her, punch her to see if she would bruise. Kiss-curls fell over her brow, you saw the tip of her tongue. But she was innocent, a child, she didn't know what she was doing — but she was a rare one for boys from the start. Father's voice trembled when he caught her creeping in after dark (it seemed Father hated Ella now), but Mother wouldn't let him go near her, it was Mother who gave her the thrashing. But she grew too big for them. She was always wandering, she loved riding home on the hay cart and she'd come in with burrs in the fringes of her shawl and her eyes moony, her mouth sore from kissing. She was disgusting, and what happened served her right. For, while Doll grew older and plainer and smaller, Ella grew bigger till she couldn't hide it. Out of all her sweethearts she chose Dick Mundy — she said it was his baby (it had to be someone's, and Dick was the only one fool enough to face Father's wrath). Mother was dying, she was spitting up blood, but the row was dreadful, they wouldn't keep their voices down. Mixed with the screaming was the smell of incense plant from the hall. Musky perfume drifted from the plant's rusty plumes, as Ella screamed again that Father only minded because he hadn't had her himself.

And the years went by and death claimed them one by one: Mother and Father, Dick Mundy and Ella. Flower Hill became the Frangipani Gardens; surely the time was right for Doll to be herself — to paint out the pictures in her head, do anything she wanted . . . but she couldn't. She was like someone embalmed. She'd worn her disguise so long, so well, that her real self was lost beneath it. She couldn't stop pretending; she was possessed by a monstrous habit.

It was like being a sleepwalker — she made her fantastic pictures at night, in a dream. When she locked the door on them and went away with the lamp, she was Miss Strawbridge again, Gully water-colourist, meek and mild.

Mother and Father had preferred her that way, and she couldn't disappoint them now. For, dead, they ruled her more strictly than they ever had alive. Now, she looked in the mirror and could only see with their eyes. She heard their deadly voices speaking for her: Homely . . . not a scrap of imagination . . . doesn't feel a thing. And, wincing, she screwed up the hateful red hair tighter, she stabbed in the pins with a queer sort of joy. She was a dutiful daughter, doing it for them: dressing so dully, painting so timid. She would show them the extent of her recklessness as she pretended away her life.

Doll could only see herself lovely when she went to the secret room. Once there, facing another canvas, she stopped being in control of what she did. She took up her brushes and let feeling guide her, as she painted a goddess with confetti-dot freckles and bonfire hair.

And she did Father as he'd been in the beginning — jolly and splendid as he showed her the view from the summit. And Mother was a lady with smiling eyes and the lines round her mouth smoothed away. And Ella was an angel-child with hair to her waist, who didn't have anything to do with the butcher-boy, the stable-boy or Dick Mundy. And though the young man in the orchard would be another person now, Doll saw him as he'd been then, and went on praying he'd return.

But night only lasted for a little while. Daytime came, and life was wearisome, you grew tired of water-colours and novels.

The years kept passing and 1914 was a drought year — all these volunteers went off to the war. Doll joined the Wattle League Sewing Circle, she bought war bonds like everyone else. In the daytime a stranger was suspicious (a stranger was always a German), but at night Father said his *Wunderkind,* the Englishman murmured poems in his gentleman's voice.

And now it is a day turning into dusk, and Doll is coming down the crazy-paved path. It is summer, and the roses look nice, but you tire of perpetual glare . . . Yes, in summer Doll was always uneasy, for summer was always a cheat. You felt drowsy, bewitched by the heat; you felt queer, somehow excited, as the shivers of heat teased you; you felt anything might happen — but it never did. The light just grew brighter, the sky arched higher, till, just when you thought it safely far away, the blueness swooped, it fell upon you, and the sky was an upside-down teacup and you were caught inside — you hit at the shiny blue porcelain hardness, but you couldn't escape (sometimes Doll hated summer — in summer you could be taken with an awful melancholy; you woke from dreaming with a stale taste in your mouth). And, as well as the sky, there were weeds. In winter you could look through the window and think of them as grass — all those different greens waving silky and velvet and soft; but in summer the green turned a pale shade, creamy, and you were threatened by a host of shimmering tassels and plumes. Kangaroo-grass had queer purplish danglers; wild honeysuckle, with its terrible sad scent of weddings was everywhere . . .

And Doll is leaning on the gate, now, thinking about summer; it is dusk (day is done with, but she can't see yet with her night-time eye: she is still Miss

154

Strawbridge), and suddenly she sees the man by the coprosma hedge. He is lying in the grass she hates, showing her his poor shattered face. He is hideous, a sure dead man, lying bleeding beside the hedge. He'd dragged himself there, and Doll can't bear to see him. She runs back up the path to her snug Queen Anne retreat.

He was a man and they'd treated him so cruel. For it was a time when sausage dogs were poisoned and you changed your name from Schmidt to Smith, and he was someone who'd appeared in the Gully from nowhere — unkempt, unknown; he was always slinking about, he haunted the orchards, he'd been seen by the creek. He was a stranger, a sure German, his fate was sealed when he opened his mouth. For he talked funny, foreign; he wasn't Australian: he had it coming to him. But Doll pitied him, just as she pitied the blowfly she swatted from the wall, the turkey that made her Christmas dinner. His face was awful, his eye wept blood, but he saw her, his eye beseeched her.

In that in-between time — not day, not night — Doll was given a chance to escape Miss Strawbridge. She could be as bold and brave and unconforming as Ella as she tended him — but she couldn't. He was a monster, he suffered. The only thing to do was to pretend he didn't exist. Doll sat inside Sorrento and shivered. She sat on and on in the dark, too scared to light the lamp (if he couldn't see her, she wasn't there). In the morning when she nerved herself to look, he was gone. The grass was stained and slippery from his blood.

It had happened years ago, but she couldn't forget — she still felt the guilt. Even though she'd been right in shutting her door. For he turned into Cockroach. His bleeding eye turned glassy and he was the devil, they said — the good Gully people who judged, who knew, who lunged at him with their sticks. Someone had to serve as a scapegoat. In time of war, Cockroach had done for the Hun; now he was perfect for dirty old man.

Every town had one, and no child was safe. What Cockroach did was whispered everywhere — but who started the whisper, no one knew. It was true, though, for there was a little boy once . . . One day it would happen again.

Who were his parents, where was his past? Sometimes he hardly remembered; it seemed he'd always been alone. Childhood — what was that? Surely he had more in common with little-many-legs, the spider, residing on his mother's back; a vestment of life, guarded, transported, snugly-housed. Beginnings — and he was the bird inside its fortress of shell, the worm tenanted in its earthy chamber, the moth waiting to issue from its silken shirt.

He'd been a small sleeper, yes, but instead of nesting among moss and leaves, he liked to curl up on the drawing room carpet. But there'd been so many drawing rooms, so many carpets, for Mama kept travelling for her health. There was always a new spa; each new carpet had a different pattern: cabbage roses, fern fronds, squiggles, a great expanse of fiery red.

The red was what Charlie remembered most, for the red was there when Papa came back. His spurs were cruelly silver against it; his soldier's coat, buttoned with brassy suns, was red, too — his coat and the carpet clashed. And Charlie had been appointed Mama's protector, he'd served her all those years, but he couldn't save her now. Her back was stiff, so protesting, as the stranger's arm wrapped round it.

But you always remembered it wrong. Papa was a soldier but when he came back from India he wasn't a great war-lord. He was a disappointment (his coat wasn't red); he was a shrivelled man in black, with trembling hands. He was as much an invalid as Mama, but he didn't want Vichy or Wiesbaden. It must be England for Papa — the place you'd started from: a land where the sky cried easily, often; where home was a house covered in creeper like a beard, and the drawing room was cluttered with brass bowls from Benares, and the carpets were sad and smoky as the sky.

Home was dreary. Though it had captured Charlie, though he woke feeling miserable each morning, it didn't exist. It wasn't true that Mama sat up in bed drinking tea — and beside her was this lump in the bed, a man . . . But it was awful, shameful, and he'd been a soldier, he had a little stick and Charlie felt its whacks when he didn't keep to the rules. For life was different, now; there was a rule for everything, and Mama had turned into a stranger. She clutched Papa's arm; they were two invalids together. Their sick eyes grudged you your leap at the sky, your swift-footed flight down the drive.

Charlie's Europe had meant palm trees and sun; cathedrals and palaces and all these statues. There were princes on horseback, warriors with perfect bodies, fat cherubim, countless Christs. Europe was a world of men, while England meant sickly old women. Mama was one, Papa was another as he dragged himself round the damp garden. Even the hedge birds sounded mournful; every day it seemed to rain more.

But across the Channel there'd been cities — Paris,

Rome, Vienna — and each day meant a hundred new faces; meant the statues and waltz music and whipped cream melting into bitter black coffee. Remember, remember . . . and it was Easter in Austria and Mama wore a pearl dog-collar and a dress with hieroglyphic embroidery and Jesus had died. But he rose from the grave, and the church was all gold, there was a smell of St Joseph lilies, almond blossom was everywhere, and you came away with a blessing twig. For in churches in Austria, when Charlie was a boy, there was a custom at Easter time of taking a twig home from the church decorations as a personal blessing.

But in England the church was dismal. Though it had a fretted Gothic spire, you knelt on a threadbare cushion and the priest had a dripping nose. There was no wonder, no mystery, only this comic with his weeping nostrils. Papa's hands trembled as he turned the pages of his prayerbook, and Charlie felt lost in a forest of nerves. His body was screaming, it was tormented by worry, for Jesus had died and in England you must mourn Him all year. Dampness and greyness kept Him dead for ever; Charlie longed for the sun to shine, for Mama to be herself again — an invalid, but interesting, wih kohl-rimmed eyes and fashionable clothes. And it was Easter, but you went home from church empty-handed. Charlie kept to the rules and ate luncheon with his elbows in and felt so alone; felt such longing for a blessing twig, an almond branch.

And then he was up in his room and the miracle happened. It was a curious feeling; there was a silence that told him he was remarkable, but he was giddy, he seemed to be moving at sickening speed. And he fell and fell till perhaps he was doornail dead, but no, he was on the Riviera where the air smelled of violets and

Mama wore an orange blossom crown. And then he felt an itching in his sleeve; then he opened his eyes, and there fell into his hand a twig similar to that blessing twig he'd so much desired.

He kept the twig in his underwear drawer. He waited for other manifestations; he had the wonders planned in his mind. He longed for more proof of his difference, he waited for some voice that would tell him what to do — and nothing happened. He was filled with a terrible hate, he only wanted to die and he tried to throw himself from the window and the hedge birds were jeering as they pulled him back; they jeered worse when he scattered vests in his search for his blessing twig.

It was gone and then there was darkness, but no more miracles; then he was ill for several years. He recovered to nod gravely, to walk stooped. They were three old people living together.

Life was quiet; Charlie supposed he was content. But Doctor was a nosey parker. He listened in to Charlie's heartbeat and said: "If you want to keep him, you must send him away." Mama thought of Cousin Diosma.

There was confusion and crying as he boarded ship, but after a while it was peaceful. Though the waves kept bucking and crockery broke, Charlie's heart beat calmer, he felt better. Day after day passed away imperceptibly and he sensed a difference of climate, of time. The evenings were shorter, it grew hot. In the heat of the tropics, Charlie came alive again. He kept being improved, even though it was cold in Australia when he landed and winter in Fern Gully, where Cousin Diosma lived, seemed as damp as winter in England.

Poor coz lay like a mummy on her sick bed; she was such an invalid that she made Charlie feel in the pink of health. Colonial society was refreshing, for nothing mattered, nobody nagged. Charlie had ceased being colourless. He'd lashed out on russet shoes in London; he'd grown his hair on the voyage out. He felt like a poet as it started to be spring — as the wattle bloomed and revealed itself to be mimosa (there'd been mimosa blossom at Nice), and the sky turned a heavenly blue.

In the Gully, Charles Roche had admirers. The mamas were always inviting him to tea, and there was an artistic girl he'd met in the orchard, and an old lady who knew that a day would arrive when medical knowledge would remove all disease; when old age would be life's single door of retreat.

It would be accomplished with vegetable remedies — Lizzie Potter spoke with passion. She looked so wild she made Charlie flinch; no wonder the Gully thought her mad.

But she was wonderful, she was the strongest person Charlie had known. She was an old woman who dressed like a gipsy and lived in a tin hut, and he had never met anyone better. She was a great teacher and Charlie was honoured to know her, and he saw that Fern Gully wasn't so tolerant, after all. Lizzie was too big for it, too strange. When Charlie walked beside her, the Gully mamas looked at him askance, and (it was ridiculous — they were so ordinary, so nice) Charlie felt a twinge of fear. Their voices were soft as they bade him their usual good mornings. But Lizzie walked with him: their eyes were hard as they skidded off her. For a moment their eyes held a look that made you feel those placid Gully matrons could do murder.

Lizzie, with her rag-bag clothes and outlandish ideas, was a threat to an ordered existence. Charlie walked with her every day, and she showed him the Gully's secrets: the idiot boy yoked to his chain, the meths drinker in his humpy of bags. She led him up all these trim garden paths, and who'd believe that so many back parlours should shelter such a variety of affliction? Addled brains, crippled body, the life that had gone on too long, were hidden away with the twin poodles on the mantel, the wax flowers under glass. The Gully was Christian, caring, and an oddity mustn't be allowed to disturb a nice person's day. Sometimes at evening when the light turned tactful, you were allowed a stroll with your keeper. But by day, by dint of being unfortunate, you must be kept out of sight.

Despite being dosed with Lizzie's medicines, they stayed just the same. But the herb doctoress seemed to like them as they were; she must show them to Charlie as if they were precious. And he was an Englishman, highborn, but he stood before them and felt lowly. Stripped of all pretending, they were terrible but beautiful, and — it was absurd, it didn't make sense — Charlie was English with smart shoes and a fashionable slouch but they made him ashamed, he wanted to beg pardon for his frivolous life.

And Lizzie lent him books of botanic remedies, she confided her cures. Charlie learned that raspberry leaves were invaluable for summer complaint of children, that white pond lily was useful in disease of the bowels. She showed him wild honeysuckle flowers and sarsaparilla root and the small fern that was a sure remedy in a case of incipient consumption.

It was while he was hunting ferns that he saw the child. She was perfect, with her ringlets and snowy pinafore. And then he saw her by the creek with the freckly girl who drew. This time she wore red — such a red dress it was, and she smiled as if she knew him. She was the purest thing in the world, and she strayed into his dreaming. She overshadowed everyone else: the unfortunates and Lizzie and Diosma; even Mama in her hieroglyphic gown.

But what was wrong with him, what was he thinking of? Charlie was a grown man, and if he had to have a dream girl it should be a young lady with a swan silhouette. But there'd never been anyone vaguely like it, he'd never felt the need. The Gully mamas took him for normal, while all the time he was someone retarded, who only wanted a baby doll: bisque head with go-to-sleep eyes and April smile with two little teeth; finely formed imitation kid body, stuffed very plump . . .

And a voice he'd never heard before started speaking in his ear. And perhaps it was the one he'd longed for, the voice that would tell him what to do with his life. But Charlie listened, and the voice was cruel. "Easily undressed," it mocked. "Patent indestructible dolly, cannot be broken by the rough usage to which a doll is usually subjected."

And, against his will, Charlie felt his body get loose — it felt different than ever before. His body leapt out of his keeping, and Charlie who read lyric poetry and picked herbs and chastely loved a little girl began to be lost. A savage animal stirred deep inside him.

Perhaps it was like that — the feeling only lasted for a short time. Then there was blackness, that lasted till morning. When he woke, he lay in the bed surrounded by clumps of lilies of the valley, wet with dew.

In the orchards, by the creek, leaning against the gate that said FLOWER HILL — she was always there. And each time he saw her he could do his trick; he loved her so much he cast violets in her path. The flowers appeared out of nowhere, they were gifts to her beauty, and he would love her for ever. But then a letter came from Papa, and Charlie must take the first ship home, for Mama was dying.

He said goodbye to the child, he whispered he'd be back, and she was with him in memory all the way to England.

Mama died before he got there; Papa was just the same. But Charlie was a different person. He owned a gift he couldn't hide — for he thought of her everywhere; he was seized by his power at all manner of times and in all kinds of places. It was embarrassing (so many roses, violets, lilies, carnations, primroses and anemones appearing out of thin air): it was wondrous. Charles Roche began to be famous, he was written up in the newspapers and they called it having supposed psychic powers and tests were made at the British College of Psychic Science.

He sat at a table with the investigators watching, and was seen to sway to and fro. Under the glare of countless lights several roses appeared in his hands. Close examination revealed them to be perfectly natural earth-like products. Dew-laden, as though just plucked from the garden, they had long stems complete with thorns.

Charlie's reputation was made. As the leading and most remarkable spiritualistic medium in Europe, he sat at tables in Mayfair and Belgravia, and the better parts of Paris and Berlin, St Petersburg and New York.

When questioned, he could tell little of his faculty; he had no explanation to offer as to why such happenings occurred. He had no knowledge of the coming of the flowers until he had recovered from the trance-like state that overcame him whenever the manifestations took place. Then, unless they were immediately moved from his reach, he would snatch at the blooms and start to eat

163

them as though famished. Once he forced roses into his mouth, until the thorns so lacerated him that blood flowed.

And the ladies who were his ardent patrons dabbed their eyes, for it was symbolic, of course. For his lost little-girl love had become part of his act — he loved her so much he let her be famous, too. The antipodean angel-child was as much a legend as Charles Roche, and the ladies sighed, for it was so touching: he was hungry for a sight of her.

Charlie was Charles all the time, now. He'd become a man who was always looking in mirrors, and he took speech lessons so his voice went deeper and fruitier, more top-drawer and foreign than ever. It quivered fetchingly when he reminisced of the little girl.

He knew she waited for him to come, and sometimes it was nice to feel maudlin, to ask himself what it was that held him back. Mama was dead, there was nothing this side of the world to hold him. But there was. There was the fame that meant the cash that purchased the breakfast kippers, the lunchtime trout . . . roast chicken and Stilton, a decent claret . . . Piccadilly collar, puffed Ascot; Inverness cape, Spanish cloak.

And he would come into the room for a sitting rather languid, in the dress-clothes that signified a crack West End tailor. For a time the ladies' tiaras sparkled; then the lights went dim and music played as he waited for his trance to come (he had subdued it to come at his bidding). And now it is a particular evening, and the blackness falls as usual: he is off. But then: *Fake,* someone called; *Fraud,* cried another. But he was a clockwork dolly, he couldn't stop; the act went on till he came to the last bit, the bit they loved. From a long way off, he heard their voices — and he stuffed the petals into his mouth. But they tasted queer, they were silky . . . it was a silk rose he chewed on, and the poppy was velvet, ditto the buttonhole bunch of double violets. And now the lights hurt his eyes, and people were screaming. They called him *Imposter* and *Charlatan*. The ones who had loved him most screamed worst — in London, Paris, Berlin.

And now he wasn't Charles, not even Charlie. As Ibhar, Egyptian Magician, many times patronized by Royalty, he greeted his sitters with strange messages and drew pictures of symbolic character on a slate. He was top of the bill with the Celebrated Living Salamander and the Infant Hercules. Seraphs whispered, phantom forms flitted; a new set of locals gasped nightly as Ibhar gripped his hands till carnations sprouted from his fingers.

And had he always been a phoney, had the flowers always come out of his sleeve? He couldn't remember, but he knew he hated his life. He was sick of the stink of carbide flares and elephant crap. The circus kept moving on, and Fern Gully seemed like paradise.

He determined to return; he scrimped, he saved. As well as being Ibhar he was Professor Roche, who read palms and predicted lucky days. At last he had saved enough: at last he was over the sea and in the Hills.

But Diosma and Lizzie had died, and there'd been no angel-child for years. There was a new set of Gully mamas who didn't know him, who distrusted his accent and the cut of his cloak. And his money ran out and he camped in the bush. It was romantic, an adventure, with little hardship involved. It was interesting to taste damper and billy tea, and it was summer and thus pleasant to sleep out. In any case, the experience stayed novel, it had no chance to pall, for Charlie didn't sample it long. For there was a war on and Hills boys were getting killed.

And you didn't eat a Berliner bun any more — now that bun was a Kitchener. And you stopped buying certain sorts of sausage, and that shop where you got those lollies — very sugary, sort of meringuey, sprinkled with hundreds-and-thousands — had its windows patriotically smashed. And there was this old man — Herr Somebody-or-other — and you held him in a neck lock while your dinkum Aussie cobber painted the Union Jack on his bald enemy head. And there was this other one — always sneaking and spying — and the Gully didn't want him, he was German to his boot straps and, besides spying, he was suspected of sorcery (though who whispered it first, you didn't recall). He didn't attend church; and babies went into convulsions at sight of him; and then he was crossing a paddock and the sheep stampeded, and then you knew he must go.

They hunted him with sticks till they found him, and they cudgelled him, they knocked him down. He fell on his elbow and he stared up at them, he pleaded — for surely they were human as he. But, fallen, he saw their faces change, for his lowly state had turned them into devils. Fallen, Charlie was helpless and they rejoiced in their power — all those virtuous Gully matrons, and the butcher, the grocer, the post office clerk. It was the women who were worst; whose teeth gleamed, whose eyes glistened as they ringed their captured prey. And he remembered Lizzie and the way those women had looked at her. It was his lost little-girl love he'd come back to the Gully to find, but Lizzie's name was on his lips as they moved in to enjoy their kill.

But when they left him, he didn't die. The quivering pain kept leaping to life, it kept him alive. It was a knife that kept striking, it screamed in his ear; it dragged him on, and everything was red.

Charlie's flayed face spurred him on towards the one safe place. He dragged himself through forests of grass, over creeping stems and lion-tooth leaves, veined petals, polished berries, sticks and stones. And he reached the hedge, he lay beneath it; and now Lizzie was with him — the grass was kind, so cool and silky, as it fanned his face. Dusk fell, a moon like a white horn rose in the sky, and small insects nibbled his hair, winged bugs drank his blood, but somehow the pain had stopped mattering.

And the woman came down the path to lean on the gate. And she saw him, she went away, but he didn't know.

As dusk merged with night and the horned moon turned a sharper white, there were rustlings and stirrings, faint whispers. The lane was mazed with shadows — and who were they, what? They stole out from behind trees and bushes; some crawling, dragging, pulling themselves forward, even as Charlie had approached the hedge. Others hobbled, shambled, limped. There were so many of them, so strange in appearance. Some were tall and sullen as thunder; others were small, with owlish faces. They were old and young; they were ageless. Club foot, hunched back, drooling mouth — all were here.

Charlie Roche had been kind to them once. He'd gone away from the Hills and come back so changed that the proper people didn't know him. But the outcasts remembered. He was altered, but he was the same man who'd walked with Lizzie; a man without the dainty nerves that ensured you must wince and flinch from the awkward reality of that Tom o' Bedlam eye, that too naked face. So when Charlie suffered they came to his rescue. Night was their time. Day kept them captive; daytime meant they were the Gully's unfortunates and freaks, its accidents of birth and circumstance. By day they were cowed and enfeebled; half-things to be hidden away or smuggled about. Yet, by night, hooked hand and great black boot; wolfish glance and swollen head — every imbecility of body and mind — turned noble. Night counted the outcasts among its beautiful monsters. Misshapen as trees and rocks, with the rank smell of beasts, they were heroes as — leering, gibbering — they tended the bleeding man.

Part Four
The Duke and Duchess

Here they were, then, in Sydney, after stepping through a floral arch. He wore his captain's uniform with cocked hat and epaulettes and medals. She was in mauve, with feather neck ruff.

And limbless soldiers lined the streets, also paralyzed ones on wheel-beds who could only flicker an eye. But some were disguised detectives, scrutinizing for undesirables. For it was Their Royal Highnesses, the Duke and Duchess.

They'd reached civilization safely, after all those foreign places. The *Renown* made her way majestically along the coast, and the destroyers *Anzac*, *Swordsman* and *Success* convoyed her; she entered the Heads; royal salutes of twenty-one guns thundered as she moved to her Neutral Bay moorings. The harbour scene resembled a carnival at Venice. The route from the warship to the landing stage had been lined with boats, their crews dressed in rainbow colours, with ribbons attached to their oars. Whistles tootled, bells clanged; loyal subjects cheered and waved hankies.

And now box cameras blinked as the procession moved off. There was a peal of bells from St Mary's Cathedral; Wirth's Circus brought out two gaily caprisoned elephants at Hay Street, who waved their trunks in the air. Night fell, and the Rose of York was first favourite as an emblem in flame; miles of electric lamps outlined main buildings.

Sometimes the Duke looked tired, but his face lit up when he smiled (when he smiled he looked just like the Prince). The little Duchess was adorable. In mauve, in Betty blue, in softest pink.

And they went on a train trip to the Blue Mountains, and saw glimpses of the true Australia through the window: swagmen, shacks, railway camps, men on horseback. And there was fluttering flag drill on ovals, and kiddies forming more white roses and lifting their voices in welcoming song. But soon it would be farewell; soon it would be Brisbane, Hobart, Melbourne — then Adelaide.

In the Queen City of the South people were getting excited. You could learn the royal curtsy and buy Duke and Duchess teacups. And a periscope to see them with was a must; likewise a Transatlantic (Concert de Luxe) glass panel radio receiver, fully guaranteed, to hear them on the air from Canberra. If you had infant twins, one could wear a dress made of two miniature flags of Australia; the other might be frocked in a Union Jack. And a railway carriage cleaner's wife gave birth to a vocal quartet, and three were named Betty and Albert and Edward (the fourth made do with Dulcie).

Lesser things happened, too. A tiger snake bore nine young ones at the Snake Park; at the Botanic Gardens the dahlias came out. Paderewski, Poet of the Pianoforte, was billed to do a Town Hall recital. And

172

Thunder, the marvel dog, was coming to West's; ditto that other popular canine actor, Rin-Tin-Tin. While at the Wondergraph, Aussie, the Boxing Kangaroo, would soon take the stage.

And the invitations were out for the Mayoral Ball. Care had been exercised to ensure that the gathering should be decorous. Except for claret cup, there would be no alcoholic drinks allowed. The presence of any person carried with it a warrant that he or she was a desirable companion. Of course Lou wasn't going.

For she was no one, she'd never make the social page, and she didn't care. She was Lou Mundy — escaped from Girlie, and from dreaming, too. She was herself, set free, and the model nursery was out of bounds for ever. For The Frangipani Gardens was O'Brien territory, and a state of war existed, and Sorrento was the hidey-hole she'd crept into. No one could get her there. Lou was a good girl who polished and swept. The neater she made the house — each lace doily frilling out just so, the shepherdess ornament smirking dead centre on the mantel, the drawing room clock tick-tocking on time — the safer she was.

And she started to walk with her arms folded, so it wasn't apparent she stuck out in front. Which proved she was modest, not a slut at all (no, never — Girlie had lied). And she only looked at males above waist, and stopped sitting under the lemon trees with Garnet; for, apart from damp grass causing piles, the two of them together — so close, so alone — might give him ideas.

It was odd how concentrating on being good made you aware of countless possibilities for evil. The harder

Lou tried to be pure-minded, the worse were the thoughts that came into her head. You folded your arms and it was like giving yourself a secret cuddle; you walked with him and could only think of sitting down. She was all the time conscious of her body nudging a message through her clothes. And Garnet had a body, too: she thought of it as much as her own. Girlie had shown Lou evil — she was constantly aware, now, of the necessity to dodge it; she could never claim innocence again.

But there were some things it was wisest to shut your eyes to. Those paintings, for instance, in Auntie's studio. Acknowledging their presence was too hard. And the fact that the door had been open and the lamp left for easy viewing . . . too difficult, so Lou chose to forget she'd seen them. Pretending was easy . . . and even if Auntie *had* done them, she was nothing like the shameless splendid woman with autumn-leaf hair and glittering eyes. Doll's eyes behind the spectacles were mild; she was an old maid, dead and dry, who'd never dared to play heroine in her life. Entering that room had been part of an elaborate nightmare . . . though, even if the paintings really *were* there, what did it matter? No one except Lou and Auntie would ever know they existed. They'd always stay hidden away; she'd never have the guts to bring them out. All unknowing, Lou scorned Doll Strawbridge as much as Ella had before her.

Lou had changed, and Garnet wasn't sure he knew her. She was always wanting to be walking — that was one thing. But she walked so stiff; she hugged herself, sort of, and stuck her nose up and never looked him in the eye. And another thing was that the words she said — they weren't Lou's. For she talked like the bits of skirt in the books that got passed round after dark in the dorm. You read them by torch light, and he never had before, but suddenly he couldn't help it. Though it was non-sense — why did he think that? It was another girl who said "Carry me away," and "Kiss me until you've had your fill." Lou wasn't tempting him, urging him on. She was perfectly proper, with her hands hidden away in her armpits (which was an odd way to walk — why did she fold her arms like that?). She was nothing like the chorus girl who bathed in champagne before invited guests, or that other one lying with a diamond in her navel on a zebra-skin rug. Trouble with Lou was, that she was so wickedly ladylike that she lured him on bad. Her mouth was so good-girl that it had a worse effect than if it had been painted in sealing-wax red. And the way she was always guarding her bodice as if it held something precious, meant he couldn't keep his eyes off and he knew she wasn't proper at all; that behind her serene glance lurked the smouldering fire of a passionate nature. But what was he thinking of? That was the book talking for him. It was Lou he walked with . . . not the odalisque who pressed her breasts together so they made a little cup, and the eunuch poured in wine and then Garnet was the Sultan who bent over her, and started lapping with his tongue.

And, walking, he wanted to stop feeling guilty. About reading the books; about misleading her about his life. For she'd got the wrong idea; he'd given it to her, she accepted it gladly, and she saw Dad as a jolly gentle-man — Santa Claus in a sola topi, written up in the history books as good and brave, a hero who'd crossed

175

impassable mountains and given peaks and plateaus his name. But he had sick on his singlet, his breath stank; most days he lolled in the store, dreaming of gold among the dusty saddles and stock whips, the tins of bully beef. And Minnie wasn't a dear departed with a MOTHER brooch at her collar. Lou pictured her as an angel, but she'd cursed and cried to escape. For home didn't have china dogs on the chimney piece and scones coming fluffy from the oven. Home for Garnet was a pug and pine hut, with the ranges all round, inhospitable, untamed. There were wildflowers, yes, but spring was a little season, squeezed between winter that meant floods and mud, and a cruel summer that seemed endless.

Sweat trickled down, the dunny was thick with flies, the sun felt as if it would burn you up. But the leaves of the pepper tree shone silver in the light, and the gallahs were pink ghosts in the sky. He longed to go back, but he was scared Dad didn't want him. He was a lost boy, and he longed to tell Lou that his stories were lies, but she went on walking, talking about how she should start her glory box and how perhaps he might work in a bank. It didn't make sense; Garnet didn't bother to listen. Once she'd been gentle; he used to play with her old-fashioned hair and rest against her soft body. Now he wasn't allowed to touch her. Now she was hard and modern and he didn't know her. He didn't want to hurt her, to imagine her as a bit of all right. Why had she changed, why must he have those thoughts?

To Doll Strawbridge, Lou seemed just like Ella. Instead of being now it was then: the past got in the way of the present, as Lou grew bigger while Doll, who was older, shrank smaller. Lou, who was Ella, took over her life; she was going to live it for her. Even Sorrento belonged to Lou now, as she played a game of housewife with a vengeance. Doll went down the crazy-paved path to the studio, but she even felt an interloper there. She was an imposter as she dabbed on water-colour; it was day, but night-time kept intruding — she'd stopped being able to divide herself neatly in two. There was confusion in her head, now. Things had never been right since the storm.

It had been one of those sessions in the room off the studio, when Doll's brush escaped her control. On a night like that, it wasn't the past that was pictured on canvas, not even Doll's yearning for the poetic English-man or her fear of Cockroach and his glassy eye. Instead, she'd paint a present that was being lived out by others, or a future that would eventually impinge on a present of her own.

One night the story of Ella's dying went down on to canvas; not long after that, Lou and Tom announced their coming. So that when they appeared at Sorrento, Doll recognized their faces — though how she knew them, why she'd expected them to come, she didn't exactly remember . . . Once that door in the studio was locked, when it was day and Doll was Mother's good girl again, she recalled her night-time familiars only faintly.

It was like that till the storm. For that night, while the elements assaulted the Gully, Doll commenced a new picture, but when she'd finished she couldn't forget it. It was crammed with stories, but she remembered them all — a jungle and a boy escaping; a snake inching closer to a goose-girl . . . and they were running through the orchard and it was Tom, it was Lou — they were safe, and somehow Doll had helped save them, but she must

177

hurry, for soon they'd be behind the hedge. So she flung down her brushes, she took up her lamp; the pictures disappeared in darkness, and it seemed the night would end as usual, with Doll turned into Miss Strawbridge (even though, this time, she couldn't forget), with all those risky stories locked away.

But she couldn't do it. Her fingers fell back from the door knob, for that door must stay open. And it was the same with the lamp: that lamp must be left to signal its message, to summon Lou to come.

And then Doll was back in her room, and she hadn't felt so happy for years. For once, the hesitations and lost chances of logical thinking had been swept away — she'd *known* she must leave the lamp; she *knew* Lou would see those paintings.

And in the morning she went on remembering — how last night she'd been someone possessed; how, now, she was merely Auntie. And she should feel utterly muddled, hopelessly divided — but she didn't. She was two people, still, but she knew she had a chance to be one.

Doll waited for Lou to come to breakfast. On the surface it was an ordinary morning, as she stirred porridge and toasted bread. Yet her heart beat so fast and she couldn't stop smiling. It was thrilling to realize that she'd given herself away.

But Doll Strawbridge didn't matter in the least, as Lou Mundy brushed toast crumbs from her mouth that refused to say anything that counted; that even laughed away the fact that Tom and Lou hadn't stayed at The Frangipani Gardens overnight.

Doll waited humbly to be acknowledged, and felt she couldn't bear it: the waiting going on, and the feeling that each minute she grew smaller, more colourless. But

178

when, at last, the big girl deigned to notice her, Doll felt even worse. For, instead of being Lou, she was Ella.

Ella's eyes looked at Doll in the old unforgettable manner (they were sneering eyes, dismissive), and now Doll wasn't anyone. She wasn't artist or Auntie; she was no one at all.

And she'd cared so much; she'd felt wonderfully brave, so sure of Lou's understanding. Doll couldn't bear her rejection. Greyness fell, it turned darker each day, till she couldn't do anything, not even see clear to paint as Miss Strawbridge.

She supposed it was like being mad in a passionless way: the greyness, the feeling of dread; the days passing and Lou, who was Ella, looking at her, sneering, with eyes that knew her secret and called it shameful, obscene. Each day Doll grew smaller; now she was nearly invisible.

And, sitting in the wicker chair, she was terrible. By the bush like a lace tablecloth she was, with her hands hanging loose in her lap. But she was Auntie, she ought to be working; her hands shouldn't be idle, they ought to be guiding the paint brush, and her tongue should be sticking out (you always saw the tip of Auntie's tongue when she painted). But somehow all the life had gone out of her. She sat with her head bent; crouched small, she was more lifeless than the wicker chair.

Tom didn't know what to do. She hardly ate, and when the fly walked on her face she didn't bother to brush it away. Now he saw she was crying. And she was Auntie, so the hanky was up her sleeve for sure, but she didn't bother to use it. She looked pale and ill. She was

179

as much a fright as the snails on the lavatory wall or the ghost girl who'd surprised Tom by the jam factory.

It wasn't right Auntie should look like that. Apart from being out of character, the bad time was supposed to be passed. Lou was all lovey over Garnet (Lou was so much in love she hardly noticed Tom and Auntie existed); Tom had escaped school and being a Catholic. He was himself again; he could visit Charlie's hut as often as he pleased. Which was where he was off to, now. Which was why, as he went past the bush and the chair and its terrible burden, he began to feel better. Charlie would know what to do when Tom told him of Auntie's condition.

Charlie had been sent an envelope. Inside it were soldiers, all sorts. Death's Head Hussars in spiked helmets, Dragoon Guards with their drooping plumes. And there were cocked hats and scarlet tunics; shiny boots and upturned moustaches; medals and aiguillettes and braided chevrons. And he saw a plain strewn with bodies and the carcasses of horses; he heard noble fellows' death cries as the carnage went on. There were murderous volleys of grape and canister, clouds of smoke and flashing sabres, as the infantry was scattered like chaff.

It was war in all its pride and splendour. He threw the pictures down, so that the soldiers lay scattered. But they were wily, they were tigers at the spring as they stared up at him from the floor. So he must get down low, he must hunt them under the table, the chair. One by one he routed them; he ripped their grinning faces to shreds.

Yet it was he who was hunted, not they. The old man whimpered as he grovelled on the floor, for now it was another wartime, and for an instant longer the face that begged for mercy was a man's. Then the blows rained down and Charlie Roche was a monster; in the end he was so hideous he frightened them off. But someone stayed — she wore black, she was singing a hymn. Pearl Reed aimed a last kick, then left him for dead.

It had been all he wanted to do — to die, to go underground where no one could get him again. But the earth was armed with grass; and Charlie was noseless, he was eyeless, his face was lost in a veil of blood, but the grass blades kept needling, as if his face was still there. Instead of a swooning fall into oblivion, Charlie twisted tormented in the grass . . .

. . . twisted tormented on the floor, for the harpy in black kept kicking him, and each kick seemed to plant a fresh seed of hate in his mind. For how cruel Charlie's life had been. All through it, human fury had attacked him shamefully; all his life he'd been spited and mocked. And he was tired of counting his troubles as joys; of shambling through life as God's fool. He'd lost everything: Mama and the child and the applause, the acclaim, as mystic roses bloomed from his fingers. He was unknown, a nobody only fit to brew simpleton's cough cures; his sole companions were a dog and a boy who took fits. And now the hate was a flower growing inside him; now the harpy was a fair woman promising rewards. If Charlie hated enough he might have anything: roses and violets; even the child.

She'd come into his arms — his sweetie kid, his knock-about dolly, and he'd love her so much. His hands would clasp her dimpled body, and he'd rock her from side to side till she screamed her *Mama*s, her *Papa*s; till

181

her go-to-sleep eyes turned glassy, till her face was as ruined as his, and the angel child was reduced to cheap trash.

But it was impossible. Hating, loving, Charlie came to his senses. Hell was about him, its spangled flames beckoned, but he turned his face from its glare.

Evil wasn't worth much. The bright blaze melted away to a pile of cold ash; His Satanic Majesty was merely Old Horny. Girlie O'Brien and Pearl Reed had been trying to spell him for years.

They'd been clever, this time. Their wax dolls had failed to catch the man, but their paper war-lords had prised out the child. For, at sight of them, Charlie was helpless; he was something small and soft and he felt their cruel teeth sink into him. They were soldiers, they were tigers, they were Papa.

. . . in India, his tunic had been scarlet, too; in India, Papa had been a hero. He wouldn't let you forget: Delhi, and the dwindling British army occupied a ridge to the north of the city, despite the Sepoy's efforts to dislodge them. And it was Mutiny, but in the end there was a turning point — Delhi fell, Lucknow was relieved. And, up to then, the story was bearable, but he had to go on; the trembling invalid in black must relive the reality of those hearts under the scarlet tunics being steeled for the work of revenge. Charlie Roche shuddered. He saw mutineers blown away from the mouth of cannon; he heard shrieks and low groans as sabres rose and fell as they went about their fearful hewing.

But Papa had long been in his grave. And in India terrible deeds were memorialized by grass plots edged with solemn yew trees. And Charlie Roche was an old man, and the soldiers were in shreds: he was safe, invincible. He had Tom and Caesar; he must remember guardian angels and magic spectacles, and those clumsy caring fingers that had found him, that carried him away . . . Lizzie had got into their hands — their blundering fingers were soothing, and in time, against the odds, his torn face healed and the wound that had once been an eye was replaced by a smooth piece of glass.

And, healed, Charlie Roche had chosen to stay in the Hills, for it was the place where he recalled the child best. Though he knew she no longer existed, that she'd turned into another, just as he had; though a time always came when he felt restless, when he must leave the Gully to wander strange roads. For he might chance upon the woman she'd grown into; he might find, in the woman, a trace of the child.

Charlie had suffered, but his life had turned good. Lizzie had helped him to forget, to grow strong enough to become mystic and herbalist and Gully bogey-man; just as she helped him, now, to rise from the floor, to cast hate and the memory of old wartimes from his mind, as he welcomed Tom to the hermitage.

2

The funeral was over and the Tarot cards kept turning. Granma lay in the cemetery and the Black Magician leered from Girlie's hand. Bat-winged, crocodile-headed, he was a denizen of the realm of darkness, yet Girlie's hand lingered, she patted him fondly, before taking up another card.

Granma was dead. She lay coffined under reddish earth that would soon be covered by a cold marble slab. The floral tributes would be withered by then — as yet they were still freshly fragrant. Pearl's was a beauty. Tending to the spectacular. A heavenly harp, fashioned from dog's-tooth violets and bloodroot, festooned with much purple ribbon.

She was gone. Her voice had been silenced for ever, but Boy went on being haunted. There were horrors worse than Irish phantoms and mustard gas; than even Jim's dying.

That war had been real enough — your boot sinking in mud and foul smells and banshee screams. Death, then, had meant flesh exploding and warm blood streaming down as wounds blossomed like scarlet flowers. Yet entangled with the horror were the little ridiculous things — meaningless, yet so human and, in retrospect, so big: football on a frozen ground strewn with barbed wire and fragments of shells, someone shouting "Buck up, George," as the King went past; chipped potato suppers in the YMCA hut, bully and biscuits for Christmas dinner.

But here was Boy, all these years later, stranded in another wartime. And it was absurd, but it was worse than before. This time there were no ordinary interludes, no comforting snatches of warmth. Even though the drawing room table gleaming fetchingly, and Girlie and her cards were so decorative, and Brother Wells chortled fruitily as Magician and Reaper turned up.

It was nonsense, though. Why war? — what put it into Boy's head? He stood on best quality Wilton in choice calf brogues. He was safe. He was dead, quite unfeeling.

Even Gran's demise meant nothing; even the fact that, motherless, Papa played little boy lost. His old face screwed plaintive, he sought attention from breakfasttime on. Girlie must slice his bacon fine; she must scold him when he dribbled egg yolk.

Boy was haunted. The toast fingers were fed into that drooling baby mouth that had once been fierce and snapping, that had once belonged to a man. And then Pearl wiped off egg and stood the great child over the lavatory pan; then buttoned him up and saw he was fit to be let into the drawing room. Sometimes Mr O'Brien pedalled dreamily at the player piano; mostly he sat watching Girlie as she spread out cards, as she shuffled them away.

Boy lit a cigarette. "Valencia" started off again on the

phonograph; Pearl mixed another batch of cocktails. It was harmless enough. He couldn't care less; he didn't feel a thing.

Liar. He shivered inside. Despite his stylish suit he was naked, utterly devoid of protection. Silk socks and golf cuff-links were no good as charms against evil.

And yet the Tarot cards made a swishing sound, peaceful, as she packed them away. And the old man fallen asleep on the ottoman was merely Papa. And it was Girlie, it was Pearl and Swells — a trio you so much despised, that they might as well not exist — who drew their chairs together; whose voices were tender, almost loving, as they said their words of hate.

Yet he wouldn't hear them — he couldn't. They had their rôles, he had his. Life was a small thing, meaningless; the days slipped away easily, without much pain, so long as you kept to your part. Boy loathed them, but usually he didn't see them. He was just as invisible to them.

The boy-hero stood at the window and tapped ash from his cigarette, but they spoke gaily, unguardedly, as if he wasn't in the room.

. . . and Hazel Teakle must be got rid of. The farce had gone on too long. She'd stopped being entertaining. Now she was too tired-making for words . . . And Doll Strawbridge, poor old half-wit — but a start had been made on her already . . . And Lou Mundy, brazen hussy . . . And Cockroach . . . And Tom . . .

Suddenly what they said mattered. They spoke of the child, the boy who used to visit. He used to walk in the garden with Girlie; he'd pushed Gran's Bath-chair down the Gully Road.

And she'd told him the Irish stories; she'd frightened him as much as she'd frightened Boy. He called out and they dragged him away; they locked him in Pearl's dark room. But Jim had been there; Jim, who loved Boy, had saved Tom from harm.

Boy's hands were trembling and the cigarette had burnt itself away. Time had passed, but he didn't know how. Their voices were still plotting, planning, and it didn't make sense — how did he know about Tom?

His body felt fuzzy, floating, and it felt as if Jim was with him. It was Jim who made Boy listen. He heard every word they said, and it was hideous. They spoke of Tom who didn't seem any different from the child Boy O'Brien had been.

Things began to happen.

Hazel Teakle killed herself and Caesar died, too. Of course, all the Gully knew about Hazel — how she cut her throat with the meat-knife, though the butcher said it was her wrists, though the post office lady had to be awkward, and swear strychnine was involved. But however it was done, she did it, and the jam factory stopped work for a day.

Caesar, though — only Tom knew about that. Charlie looked at him strangely, that day when he reached the hermitage. And the dog was just lying there, stiff, with the ball Charlie used to throw at him to jump for, stuck in his gullet. It had happened before — Caesar jumping for the ball so excited, with such violence, that it got stuck. But always before he'd put his head down and give a few heaves and out it would come. This time it hadn't — he couldn't bring it up. The ball stayed down and Caesar died. Tom watched, while Charlie had another go, and somehow got it free. But what came

187

out, all foamy, wasn't Caesar's softish rubber ball. This ball was harder, heavier, though Charlie hadn't noticed it when he made his throw. Tom felt uncomfortable, it was awful seeing Charlie like that: gathering Caesar in his arms, sobbing.

Well, these things were trying, it was all rather sad. But Caesar was only a dog — a mongrel, at that, and Hazel, poor thing, had been weak in the coconut for ages. These things happened, but they didn't much matter.

What did, was that Lou had her hair cut. She decided all of a sudden. One minute she was dusting Auntie's shepherdess ornament, the next she had this feeling that she couldn't stay in the house. It was as if she'd smother if she didn't get out of Sorrento, and she couldn't bear the feel of her hair hanging floppy on her neck. She knew she'd go mad as Hazel if she couldn't have a shingle; if she didn't get away from Tom's moony eyes and Doll sitting in the drawing room in a little pool of dust. She was in the way when you swept the carpet, she wouldn't move her feet. Auntie was someone Lou couldn't ignore, since she'd chosen to come in from the garden.

She was creepy. Like a fly with no wings, or the white puppy that squirmed on the road till the man came to hit it with a brick.

Life was meant to be charming, and Lou was being cheated. She threw down her duster and went to Auntie's drawer; she knew she had every right. If she'd stayed at the Bon Marché to be a shop girl there would have been regular pay-days. She felt virtuous as an avenging angel as she opened Auntie's hanky box where she kept the neatly folded pound notes. She knew she was off to town. There was just time to catch the morning charabanc.

And all the way in, as the Hills sped by, she felt in a trance. She couldn't stop smiling, as she savoured the secret. How on the outside she was merely Lou Mundy — fat, with old-fashioned hair. A sensible girl who anticipated a house with rockwork and china frogs in the garden; whose first finger left was nearly pricked raw from all that sewing for her glory box.

But in secret, inside, Lou was quite someone else. Hot jazz melodies bloomed in her head, and it was autumn, but she was tormented by spring. She felt as tempted as a heroine of Miss Corelli's; she didn't care if she ended up like Lillian Gish in *Way Down East*, being turned out into the snow by her stern papa.

Lillian had a baby without being married, and it was a film Ella used to cry in. Lou snuggled against her, and started sobbing, too, as she bit on her ice block from interval. The piano vamped worse and your plush seat was soft. Your teeth ached from their bite on ice; the tears spread warm on your cheeks . . .

In Adelaide, flags and pennants waved from every point of vantage; triumphal arches were going up everywhere. For Their Royal Highnesses were almost come. Hotels were full, boarding houses crowded. Visitors, finding accommodation difficult to obtain, were sleeping two and three in a room.

It was a fairy-tale city and Lou had the feeling that some of the magic was laid on for her. She had money in her purse and something good was going to happen — she would return to the Gully with curls like question marks on her cheeks and her coat collar rubbing a freshly shaved neck.

The shop window dummies wore satin and lace. Though, as well as evening frocks, there was all this fur wear. For winter approached — even the Duke and

Duchess couldn't keep it away. You'd soon need that coney coat, that stole of skunk opossum. There were rabbit skins, squirrel skins, marmot skins, wolf skins — so elegant and excellent, so smart and cosy. But they were dead, dead, dead. The worst one was the fox with its little dangling paws. Its glass eyes stared. Girlie had a fox fur like that.

And now Lou was inside the biggest of the big shops. And she must hurry from counter to counter; she must purchase lippy and powder and scent (and should it be Russian Violets or La France Rose?). It was as if she had a fever; even as she waited to be served she had a feeling of panic that only a counter away was the best buy of all — if she didn't get a move on she'd miss it.

She must have the *crêpe de Chine* hanky, the shadow silk stockings; the velvet poppy, the sequin ornament. And then she was going up in the lift, and so many ladies crammed tight together smelled strange. There was a smell of wild beasts under the icing sugar smell of cosmetics.

Some ladies were going up to the Tea Gallery and Roof Garden with its glorious view of the city's scenic environs. But Lou got out at the Beauty Parlour, where all ravages of climate and age might be removed.

It was Hairdressing, too, and you didn't need an appointment. Next thing, Lou was sitting before a mirror, and she hadn't known it would be done by a man. She felt embarrassed as he bent over her, his hands intimately brushing her neck. And then it was like murder: just a few cruel snips, and her hair was all over the floor.

She felt trembly as she got ready to meet him. It was thrilling pulling on the stockings and smoothing her eyebrows with spit. She pouted, so her underlip resembled a shiny cherry; she had a second dab of Russian Violets, for it would be a let-down if he didn't catch the scent.

And he was there by the lemon trees, and so overcome by her appearance that he didn't know what to say. They started walking and he seemed scared to touch her — even her hand. Leaves fluttered down; autumn flowers were everywhere. Soon Lou's silky legs were powdered with pollen, flecked with winged seeds.

They stumbled, separate, through soursobby orchards. Teakle's wouldn't have bothered with these trees. The peaches and apricots were given up to curl-leaf and spot-hole; the apples were full of codlin moth.

Garnet was a stranger, struck dumb. It was crazy, fantastic, and Lou gave herself up to the dream. He led her through a forest, an enchanted wood. They went in and out of sun and shade — now your eyes were crinkled, fighting the light; now they were blinking, trying to see in the dark. Leaves crumbled away under their feet. The trees loomed and it grew darker; then the leaves came untangled, they seemed to be burning, and the light was smoky before it went gold. They linked hands and started to run. He loved her, Lou knew, though his face was so set, so strange.

They crashed through the grass together. Branches see-sawed, something secret scurried away. And now the apple trees were familiar, for they'd reached the orchard that bordered the model nursery. There was a smell of wet flowers, a sound of water flowing. The bushes looked furry, like caterpillars; leaves stuck out like hands that wanted something from you.

191

Suddenly they were standing still. He looked at her and started laughing as he ran his hands through her hair. He laughed, and she couldn't bear it. She tried to push him away, but the grass laced her feet, it tripped her up. He fell with her, and for a moment they lay quiet; they were tender as their bodies tilted together.

But then the grass went bruised. They were fighting and hitting and the sky slid sideways and now it wasn't day but night. He lay over her and blocked out the sun and she cried out for him to go on. Her body went careless, she wanted anything to happen. She was so big, she was just like Ella.

They folded close, to make a big pale animal. You must fondle it, feel. Some parts were silky-smooth, others were fuzzy as the skin of a peach, and there were hanging bits like queerer fruit.

And now it was happening fast, now it was slow. It went on and on and tears were all over Lou's powdered face for it hurt before it was beautiful. And she pushed her body at him, for she never wanted it to stop, but they started to come apart; her skin slipped away from his fingers.

Then they were dolls. They lay separate, sprawled, and Lou opened her eyes to see clouds making a tree in the sky; and the rayed sun was a flower, there was a wrinkled moon pressing close, too. It was a scene just as perfect, as pretty, as a Tarot card picture. This face like a moon seemed to think so, as well. It watched them hard; it watched them with a queer flushed smile. He was hidden in the bushes but Lou saw him. One eye was gloating; the other stayed cold, unmoved, because it was glass.

3

The soldiers kept coming and his eyes made him look. He didn't bother to tear them up, now. When he tore them, his fingers turned sorry; they must play paper chase over the floor, then get out the Tarzan's Grip glue, and stick till the soldiers were mended.

Resurrected, they were worse than before. Somehow the wrong bits were always united. Blue tunic, scarlet-faced, buttoned up to workaday khaki; shiny black boot clicked against Blancoed shoe; feathered cocked hat merged with Kilmarnock bonnet.

He'd been sticking so long and with such care and he'd only succeeded in making comics. All their dare-devil swagger, their hostile beauty, had ended up merely ridiculous. Faces were splintered with tear marks like rapier wounds, stale glue dribbled like sweat from beneath the spiked helmet; and you were young and old at the same time, your smile began smooth and finished jagged. Instead of being a hero, perfectly brutal, you were reduced to a rickety monster.

And Charlie hated them, he loved them. They were Papa, they were the Duke — he was so muddled.

For there were always new pictures, and now they'd stopped being anonymous; now they were always of one man.

But the Duke was every inch a sailor. He wore captain's uniform and the royal train had brought him from Melbourne, and as he stepped from the carriage the Artillery Officer telephoned "Fire". So that as the Duke's foot touched red carpet the first shot of a twenty-one gun salute boomed out.

And autumn sunshine came crisply from pale blue skies, mingling deliciously with a south-westerly breeze that stirred the bunting. And there was martial music and the triumphal progress started off, the troopers' white horses trailed dung. All Adelaide cheered and the Town Hall bells chimed. People tip-toed, they stood on tables and step-ladders. Pink-stockinged legs (looking dreadfully nude from a distance) made a fringe along the roof of the Post Office, where flappers sat on the parapet and defied nerves.

Charlie didn't understand. There must be a reason for the newspaper cuttings. With the one headlined ADELAIDE'S SUNNY WELCOME was one telling what happened in '68. Then it was another tour, another Duke, and the Fenians plotted assassination. But though the bullet felled H.R.H., he recovered to live. A wave of relief passed over the continent and the miscreant was hanged and was it supposed to happen again? But Charlie didn't have a gun — was he meant to play David with a stone? He couldn't be sure. He wished his head didn't hurt; he wished he wasn't alone.

Caesar had died. He stretched his neck to snap at the ball and it was a lively bouncer (Caesar smiled as it gripped his teeth), but instead of being india-rubber, a ball that would not injure, it was heavy — like a big marble, a large spangled knocker, a glass tiger, a Yankee steelie — and it kept going down: till it stuck.

And Charlie wanted to cry but he started to laugh. He was so alone, and he had to get away from his house. Someone had switched balls, and he couldn't sit lonely without giving vent to his feelings. He kept crying and laughing, and seeing Caesar half-choking, then choked. And the soldiers kept advancing, and the Duke had come, and what was Charlie to do?

But when he left the hermitage, the wind tried to drive him back — it swirled his cloak, it spun him round — and the herbs clutched his feet, but he trampled them off, so that herby smells blended together. And the bees swarmed and clustered, so he must play scarecrow and waggle his fingers; he must ape St Vitus dancing with angels. And he threw his head from side to side like the mad Bible king, for it was a man hunt and all nature was out to get him.

Things rushed and ran, they came in scurrying surges — they were ants and beetles and queer red bugs, and something hissing through the leafy tunnel. It blew hard enough to puff him back home, but Charlie persisted. He vaulted pits and trenches and the grass jostled him — it was green and waving and dangerous as a sea full of snap-toothed sharks — but Charlie pursued his solitary path and at last the Hills turned calm.

Now everything was comical in the extreme, and Charlie started to sing. He sang: "Oh where, oh where is my little dog gone? Oh where, oh where can he be?" Nothing mattered, for Charlie had braved chasms, forests, bogs, morasses, mountains and now it was a marshland . . . but, no — it only reminded him of that because everything was grey: sky, gum trees, fence posts, grass. But then the sun returned; it shone in his eyes, sparking and tinselled, till Charlie must wince with pain as he remembered how she was a pretty little thing, a dear, and he gave her violets and roses, and everywhere he went she was with him, even in old-fashioned lands where icicles were hanging daggers and snowflakes whirled like white bees. But he lost her in modern times. But Charlie blinked away the tears — for, not to worry, she was somewhere ahead.

He was on his way to find her, even though there was magic and witchcraft about. He was in among the twisty apple trees, and there were sucking sounds for the creek was near. Charlie went on and on, past the shadows of the willows, and now he'd come to her orchard. Her house was up the top of the hill and she'd run down to meet him and for so long he'd sought her, he'd kept himself pure, and now here she was. But it was sad, for she made it seem easy, as she held out her arms. Charlie couldn't watch. He hid behind the bushes and, hiding, he missed out on his turn.

Someone else took her. Her skin filled a stranger's fingers; her body burst into his hands. And she had tricked him, for she wasn't a child at all. She was a big girl, a woman, and the boy threw her down. Now Charlie must look. He felt sick but he must see: their bodies stuck together like pink nougat pieces, the sweat moustaches above their lips. Then his face went over hers like a mask, and in their armpits were little furry animals, and it seemed they did cheek-to-cheek dancing, lying down.

The light swam and trembled, midges veiled them in a gauzy tent, but nothing could hide what they did. Charlie shivered. He felt as if he watched them through a pane of icy glass. They were locked in a warm fleshy world, while he was left out in winter for ever. They were together but Charlie was alone, and he hated them, he wanted to sing about a lady who kept a wonderful tomcat. And root-to-to-too-e-e-it! — didn't they go at it; wasn't he a regular slobberlips.

Oh, but it was disgusting and they were only two kids, yet rooting like they could never have enough. At last they fell back. The galanty show was over and they lay loose as puppets on the grass.

And all through the Hills, boys were running. They were boys from Fern Gully College, but they'd taken off their Roman Catholic clothes. Now the boys were disguised in khaki, and they had knotted hankies round their necks and soldiers' hats; shoulder patches, name tapes and badges.

These boys were Boy Scouts and Tom wished he were one, too. A Scout knew the secret sign and did a good deed a day and was always smiling. Scouts could tie reef knot and clove-hitch and fly the Union Jack; they were wise fellows who didn't scatter toffee papers and would end up with money in the Savings Bank. Now they were out here, running about. Tom watched them nicking tree trunks, consulting the compass, arranging arrows from sticks and stones.

It was like a club, and everyone was in one but Tom. If you weren't a Boy Scout you could be boy and girl together like Lou and Garnet, or you could give up like Doll and sit tight till you belonged to your chair. Everyone belonged to something, everyone had their label. You were a Catholic or a boy-hero or a hermit — Tom wasn't anything at all. Once he'd had Charlie who'd said they were equals; but when Caesar died, Charlie Roche changed. You couldn't tell him about Auntie any more, for he'd turned into Cockroach; he'd become the hermit he was supposed to be. And a hermit belonged to aloneness, so Tom must be frightened away.

Cockroach waved his stick, he spoke foreign. His glass eye spat fire and he was the gipsy who'd steal you, the sandman who'd send you to sleep. He was as bad as the wind that could freeze the grimace on your face, or the falling star that meant a dead baby.

Tom had left the Scouts behind. He was out of the gum trees and into the orchard and up there was The Frangipani Gardens and down among the apple trees was Charlie . . .

And since he'd seen her play harlot, nothing counted. It was all he could think of: her baby flesh growing bloated, turning wickedly womanish before his eyes. One minute she was innocent; the next, spinko-spanko, she was ruined.

Charlie had wanted to kill her, but somehow she got away. She did up buttons like a mad thing, she hid herself in a grown-up disguise. The gentleman stayed reclining on the grass. Charlie could have killed him easy.

But bow-wow-wow, it was angel-child he was after, and damme, if he didn't feel her hand on his sleeve. It seemed like her; Charlie thought it was her. It felt like little girl's hand, though the eyes and the hair were different . . .

And Tom touched him, he shook him gently, for it seemed that Charlie must be asleep. Though *was* it Charlie? — Tom couldn't be sure. The skin was right — splintered and wrinkled; the eyes were Charlie's, too. But the spirit of the man was missing . . .

And the child kept pestering him and it wasn't a girl but a boy, it wasn't the one he wanted. But it had a child's flesh and its smell — milksop mixed with the sweaty scent of new pennies — was perfect: little girl had smelled like that.

Charlie mused; he sat mum, and felt the dizzy pleasure creep upon him. The child's smell, its fingers, had stirred an old animal to life. Charlie's body stopped being sawdust-stuffed; now it was inhabited by a nightmare wolf. The child was a silly, it would deserve all it would get. The animal was savage with a fury's temper, but the child kept petting it on.

And he wouldn't care what he did. He would let the animal have its head. For so long Charlie Roche had been hated and feared; he'd been treated as a foe by the Gully. He was tired of playing wise man, of keeping himself good.

But Tom loved Charlie and he started to fight. Fighting was like having a fit. It was being a golden eagle and beating at Charlie with your wings, assailing him with your great cutting beak.

Tom twisted and writhed and grasped Charlie's stick. He raised it in tender violence, for he loved Charlie so much he would kill him, he would do anything to free him from the devil beast's grip. But he didn't have to bring the stick down, for at the sight of it Charlie was cowed. He was no longer a tiger who'd munch away your arm to the elbow; now he was a captive circus beast, enfeebled and mangy.

Tom ran towards the smell of sausages and chops. It was lunchtime and the Boy Scouts were hungry; they squatted round the campfire and sang a song about a kookaburra, and waited for the billy to boil. But Tom belonged to no club, he ran on . . . and here is a Scout lost in dreaming, still arranging sticks into arrows; and here is a Christian Brother, walking along very stealthy

... They didn't see Tom, they were coming together, and the Boy Scout had better watch it, for Swells was a worst beast than Charlie.

4

And Doll Strawbridge was real, she existed. Each morning she climbed from bed, and next thing her night-dress was a tent with her head sticking out, and inside the tent her hands dressed her body, they helped her legs step into the parts that weren't mentioned. It was all done so modest, and at last the undies were on, and ditto a Queen Mary dress.

And she kept her head steady, she didn't jut or strut, or throw her arms out as if she was flying. And her eyes behaved, too. They didn't wink or cast about, but stayed reserved. And so she reached the dining room and for a while the others were there (but she only saw them as shadows). And she sat at the table and used her spoon right (Mother said Good girl as Doll took porridge from the side of her spoon). And if you ate fruit tart you used a fork as well, and the spoon was raised to the mouth for the purpose of receiving fruit stones. Though strawberries might be taken up by the stalks in the fingers. Though pears, apples, peaches and nectarines were eaten with a fruit knife and fork.

Fruit was a good subject to think on. Doll thought on it all day and into the night. Now and then the shadows moved about her, but she didn't much care. She only heeded Mother's voice talking in her head, telling how grape pips weren't ejected direct from mouth to plate; how oranges were divided into quarters, and each quarter was peeled separately as required.

And if fruit didn't suit, you could consider the etiquette of introductions or visiting cards. There was so much to ponder, and now Doll was in the drawing room, sitting on her spindle-leg chair. Sometimes the big girl dusted round her, but she wasn't here today. Doll was free of her, and of the staring boy, too.

She used to sit in the garden. But on the quince tree was an insect. It had twitchy legs and a St Andrew's cross on its back. And it was nervous, all quivering, it was scared worse than Doll. For the nasturtium leaves were big and the butterfly skipped; daisies flapped and zinnias blazed. And didn't the lawn grow fast, and there was so much grass in the lane. Oh dear, grass and the lane meant Cockroach. His eye was in every daisy, his blood in each fuchsia bud that begged to be popped.

So she sat with the Chippendale clock and the gate-legged table of fumed oak. Perfectly still she sat, perfectly ladylike, and she was as thin as a whipping post; she should be fed on mutton pies and German sausage. Care had forcibly written its lines on her face; she looked cold and blue, pinched and pecked. She was a lost lady from another age; she should be put to bed with a bag of hot sand and a sip of wine negus.

Poor Doll. The curtains hung by rings on a brass rod, the table was daintily occasional; there was a parlour palm and a crested ribbon fern. And on the wall was a floral frieze and the water-colour paintings were ornamental, and Doll did them, but she doesn't paint now. She just sits. She is the deadest thing in that room where good taste is a guiding spirit.

She was like a frozen person. She was benumbed with cold, she was terribly nipped. It was as if her blood was so cold it formed a solid clot; as if all the little blood vessels were choked and swollen, and the circulation was quite stopped.

But suddenly she started to change. She thought of fruit in a different way — she thought of how diarrhoea was said to come in with the plum season, and she thought of the cherry plum tree at Flower Hill and how Mother used to tie her cherry plums in muslin bags (but the birds still got them). And Doll was a child again, and it stopped being the sleep of death. Suddenly it felt as if someone started to rub her alive with a teaspoonful of dry mustard and an ounce of lard, which was Mother's favourite cure for chilblains. And it always used to work, and Doll felt so strong, and nothing could make her afraid. Not even the occasional table and the escritoire.

For the furniture took frightful shapes. Instead of being inlaid and smooth, the wood was shaggily patchwork: it was bark, it was the trunk of a tree. And how funny the jardinière and the standard lamp looked, stranded among them . . . but then they were gone, as well. Then it was only the Hills and gum trees were everywhere and was it a picnic? For Mother spread the tablecloth, and you peeled the hard-boiled egg, you nibbled the chicken leg, but then Doll must wander on. She must go where there were apple trees and she saw the pink people like Adam and Eve and she saw the child in the old man's arms. And he was struggling, and at first Doll was just watching him, but next thing she started to be him. She was a boy not a girl: she had got into his body, she was fighting for his life. And the boy screamed and ran wildly, and he led her where there were soldiers. But it wasn't the Bush Contingent, off to South Africa in ostrich plumes; it wasn't a battalion of Anzacs. These soldiers were only pretending as they wiped up sausage grease with bread. And then Tom Mundy was nowhere near, and Doll Strawbridge painted as never before.

She was in among the gum trees, but she was also in her studio. And the secret room was unlocked, but she wasn't painting inside it. The door of that room was open and the pictures spilled out: love pictures, where Doll was a wanton with tumbled hair and blue-faced baboons chattered, love birds soared, the poetic Englishman conjured up his flowers.

It is daytime and Doll has come alive. She escaped from the drawing room and seized a new canvas and took up the paints — the sticky ones that smell excited, the ones she must squeeze on in worms and mould with her hand. And the pink girl and boy twine together, and in the bushes crouches Cockroach and Tom Mundy is captive in his arms, but the eagle plunges and Tom gets away and next Doll paints in the Scouts and the sausages sizzling nicely and the kookaburra song they sing. But then Doll doesn't want to paint it, but she must. Oh why is this Boy Scout so innocent, oh why is he little and trusting? Jesus winks silver and the rosary beads jingle and the Christian Brother's fingers keep moving. Swells is quite as gentle as a woman in his touch, quite as thoughtful about little wants — yes, really far more tender and considerate than any woman. It is a nice thing he does to the Boy Scout. A man's strength is a great advantage. And Doll cannot do anything but paint. This is a boy she cannot help. But it was over very soon.

Lou and Garnet were two people, now. The big animal they made in the grass came apart, and Lou threw on her clothes and ran up the slope. Instead of Russian Violets there was an onion smell from under her arms. She could smell her body as she ran. She was shameless, she had let him do it.

The thing had happened as it had always been meant to, for Lou had never been free. From the start she'd been an outcast; she was a poor girl with Ella for a mother. It was like being born a mechanical doll — she'd smiled and nodded on cue, as invisible hands wound her up. She was sure to be in the duff, up the spout. Those ladies in town had said it all along — it happened to girls like Lou Mundy.

She'd been another Ella from the day she was born. She'd never been anyone else. She had Ella's body and her face, and she went to town and had her hair cut and just when she thought she was proper, she was Ella worse then ever, more and more.

And she was at the gate that said FLOWER HILL. But it was The Frangipani Gardens, now, where exotics grew and probably it was the only place to go.

Then something made her turn round, and she saw Garnet at the bottom of the slope. The apple trees were round him like a cage; he was a schoolboy, and Lou couldn't help but love him. And she knew her life was ruined and that his father wasn't anything flash, and that Garnet would never be, either. Lou would never have romance or a Grand Rapids carpet sweeper. There'd always be dirt and babies crying.

Doll's hand holds the paint brush and it is like riding a bike with no hands. Once you get started it is easy. No hands — and the wheels spin along, spinning you with them. Painting, Doll's style, is similar. Though her hands hold the brush she doesn't have to look. It is as if someone else does the painting for her. The brush knows where it must go; it knows what story it must tell.

And so Lou is made to turn back, and now Garnet and she are together. It is a good bit to paint, so Doll is happy, but the picture is nowhere near finished. There are so many bodies swirling out their patterns, it is such a muddle that Doll wonders if the picture will ever be done.

Now she is painting faster and faster; now she smears on paint with her fingers. The paint is like mud, like blood. And it is a new picture Doll paints, and this time she doesn't want to look. For by the creek lies a little dead soldier.

The child's body is so small, and only a brute could have done it: it was Cockroach who did it, of course. The Christian Brothers cross themselves; they are united, now — the Irish sweaty ones, the ones with Spanish-saint faces. Brother Wells's fingers flicker grace-fully — he has beautiful hands, so white. Swells says more prayers than anyone. He takes it hard, for he liked that Boy Scout.

And after the praying they start off down the Gully Road. As well as the Brothers and the Scout leader who found him, there are all these Gully mothers and fathers. It is teatime, but the tablecloths stay folded away, as people approach the orchards from town. They make an army. Now they have left the road. Their sticks swish briskly as they stride through the grass.

They hate him so much; they have been waiting so long for this day. It was Cockroach who was to blame when the milk went sour and the Iceland poppies were taken by the frost. He was at the back of everything bad and he kept a black sheep with curly horns that would jump on any lady at her time of the month. And his thumbs were turned in, which was Satan's sign, and of course none of it was true — they were just stories, just part of your childhood. But surely he knew what you felt when you saw him? Surely he knew how little you were under your grown-up disguise? And you hated him for doing it — for making you feel naked and no one at all — and you loved him, too, and would see him thrashed raw. And once a dove came out of his mouth, and his house was made of bread with windows of sparkling sugar. And his house was a handsome structure in late Gothic style. And his house was a blackfellow's wurley. And they would find him, they would hunt him. The Christian Brothers hitched up their skirts; they got down low, for now they were up to the tunnels.

But they were nothing much, you needn't crouch long, for the tunnels were mostly trampled away and there was no dead baby snared on the thorn bush. Every twist and tangle had been clawed from the undergrowth; there was nothing to frighten you, not even a swarm of wild bees. Someone had driven them off; they throbbed with anxiety high above your head — they were as scattered as fern seed and soon it would be the dark cold months and the queen would doze away, comatose as a hibernating bat. And the herb garden was plundered, it was a sad broken place, but they were almost there: they fell silent. You heard the sigh of skirts and the silvery sounds of beads and smelled, mingled with the stench of dying herbs, a stink of fear.

For he had a face like a dissected puzzle and a glass ball for an eye and yellow leaves fluttered down, there was a storm of veined petals. Someone had stirred up a wind to shake away the last dregs of summery autumn and he was the devil and his beard was snapdragon, stinkhorn was his member, and Brother Wells was brave, he was first at the door.

But the house was a cheat. There were no gingerbread shingles, no Gothic gables, no woven wattle twig walls. It was merely a wooden hut and the door wasn't locked. They didn't have to knock it off its hinges, they weren't allowed dramatic gestures. Brother Wells just turned the knob and they followed him in, and found they'd been cheated worse.

They raised their sticks, but he wasn't there to bring them down on. Cockroach had scuttled off; he'd only left their sticks the bottles of stimulants and sudorifics, tonics, diuretics, astringents, vermifuges, nervines, purgatives, expectorants and demulcents. It was poor reward for their coming, but the tinkles were lovely, and they went mad and smashed the Nondescript and the Jap Mermaid, too. But it wasn't enough, and it was Swells who struck matches and made a bonfire of the paper soldiers. Pips and polished boots, spurs and medals blazed and a goliath beetle ran across the room and the devil's coach horse galloped after it, and that beetle would lead you to whoever you sought (it was

208

another childhood story, and one you believed). So they threw themselves at it, they all rushed out and Swells, who was first in — he came last. And somehow he tripped. His gargoyle face smashed on slivers of glass, he fell in a small stream of carminative tincture that was useful for female debility. And dill seeds got up his nose, angelica root slipped in at his mouth, he had sprigs of motherwort in his hair. And the fire fed on books and dried herbs, and it leapt at his priest's dress and he lay there with his dog lips smiling and his white hands spread wide.

Now Brother Wells is burning. His eyes are open, they look astonished, as his body is wrapped in a fiery cocoon.

5

It was night, and white flowers were open in Doll's garden. They scented the air; their white petals beckoned.

Moths were everywhere. They circled, they flew swiftly as birds. Their wings made a humming noise, as they hovered over the bed of evening primrose.

In the sky the stars were so thick they looked tangled. Some were clustered to make silver arrows, and there were wisps and tassels making a ragged scarf. The stars looked so close together, yet Charlie had said there were great gulfs between them; and that between them and us lay a dark abyss of space.

Charlie was lost to Tom, now, he was as far away as the stars. Out in the garden, tears pricked Tom's eyes. He was alone. Behind him, the windows of Sorrento glowed, and Garnet and Lou were together. In the studio Auntie painted on.

Some stars made a river that spread itself in shallows, that narrowed and were almost lost. Sometimes the sky was knotted and streaked; dark channels appeared in it, and holes of blackness. Tom stared and stared — he felt safest doing that — but the tears kept coming, they made everything strange. It seemed that his crying eyes looked through stars into the space beyond them. It seemed he looked on the beginning and end of space, and the black hole of nothingness came nearer, and the night sky started to whirl.

He was alone and he always would be. He was different from everyone, he didn't fit in. Once he'd been happy with King Billy and birds, but now they weren't enough. Tom wanted something more. Once he'd had Charlie for a friend; now that he'd lost him all his old contentment was ruined.

Tom had ceased being a boy safe inside a world of his own. For so long he'd been snug as he leafed through the encyclopedias and dug on the cliff top for pieces of quartz. And though he left the lagoon, in the Hills he still had birds. It had been a bird that led him to Charlie; a bird that delivered him from Cockroach. But with Charlie become Cockroach, everything had changed. It was as if the glass dome of content that had settled on Tom's life — that had kept him immune from the town's taunting boys and the matrons who'd whispered behind their gloves; from Alf and Vi; from his days at The Frangipani Gardens and that night in the orchid house with Swells — had lifted. Now Tom stood exposed in a world that was foreign.

Inside Sorrento, Lou sat close against Garnet, and they were making plans for going away. In the studio Auntie kept painting, and now Tom was past the quince tree with its swag of clumsy fruit, and furry moths blundered against him. Yet nothing was real — not quinces or moths or the daffodil moon. Not Auntie applying paint with her fingers.

She painted in a dream. Tom stood in the doorway and thought she'd never stop. But suddenly she threw down the paints and ran past him. Her eyes were blind, she didn't see him.

The stars shone brightly, and the moon somehow swooped, and the quinces hung like dusty yellow lanterns. There was light all about her, and Tom saw she wasn't Auntie but a stranger. She wasn't timid and ladylike; she was still the bold artist who'd painted in the dark without a fumble, as if she was guided by God. Her blind eyes were shining, she'd left off her spectacles, her hair shed its pins to float loose. She had paint all over her fingers and it was smeared on her face — she was a painted queen jumped free of a portrait, though her dress swirled as Queen Mary's never would. Tom ran down the crazy path behind her. Where was she going, what did she seek?

And Charlie had heard the army, he'd seen their sticks as he crouched low in the grass. He was nothing, now; his body felt dead and he couldn't remember what it was he'd done wrong. There'd been a child, he thought — but who it was, but what he'd done, he couldn't remember. But their cries had been terrible, and they were out on a hunt; there were black skirts striding and it seemed like a witch hunt. And now it was his mind that was dead; it was his body that started to come alive. Charlie's body remembered and dragged him along. It crouched and crawled and took him out of the orchard. Now he was in the lane and he didn't know how he'd got there. For a long time he rested; he lay hidden in the grass with his body almost as uncaring as his mind. But then his nostrils smelled smoke, and their sticks made a memory, and fear prodded him on.

Tom stood at the gate beside her and watched the figure coming towards them. It came slow, all bent and jerky. It swayed, it stopped, it started again. Its erratic dot-and-carry-one walk seemed to suggest a peg-legged fate.

Tom shivered. A stranger approached and it was the bogey-man, for sure, but Doll Strawbridge leaned forward in welcome. Instead of staying safely hidden behind the squeaker hedge, they were silhouetted, out in the lane. The man stumped closer. Tom knew he'd have a cruel face; that there'd be a dangling butcher's knife, keen-edged, at his belt.

But Doll leaned forward, she held out her hands; she was the carved lady on the front of the sailing ship. And the man was up to them, now, and his face swam pale in the darkness and Tom saw that he was Cockroach.

Doll was smiling, soft; it was the sort of smile you showed to a lover. Tom wanted to warn her that the man was a devil, but the words were stuck in his throat.

Ages passed. He was by the gum tree, he was lost in shadow, but he was looking at them, Tom knew it. And it had to be Cockroach, but it seemed like someone else — perhaps the man was even Charlie.

And now Tom wanted to go to him. It was Charlie, and he loved him, he would forgive him anything; he wanted him inside Sorrento in a world that was safe.

But Doll held him back. He felt her hands on his shoulders; she was holding him. All the wild life had gone out of her, and she was a weight on his back. She bent over him and her hair drifted down in a soft orange cloud. Her hair was in Tom's eyes till she lifted her head, and by then Charlie had moved on.

He was an old stranger, blurred by darkness, trudging up the lane. He stalked on, a huddled shadow man; his shambling footfalls died away. For a moment more Tom saw him, then he was gone. Night took him — or that clump of trees, that bend in the lane.

And where was he going, what would become of him? Would he trudge on for ever, an old man from myth, bound for those lost cities that were part of his past, where wolves howled and snow whirled and the Fat Boy tucked into faggots and mustard pickle, and the Bearded Lady minced forward draped in a tattooed shawl? And would he find peace at last, had he found it already — slumped in tangled grass, sunk away beneath a drift of rusty leaves?

Tom held Doll's hand and they walked back through the garden. The jasmine smelled good and that rambler rose was called Maiden's Blush. The stars made a filmy lace in the sky; the feathery-plumed moths still circled. And Sorrento was so ugly, it was so dear. It was home, such a little house, and Tom was glad to be inside it.

They sat in the kitchen and Doll said she'd make some cocoa. She was hungry, she said, for she'd been painting so long. And she needed her specs to see with: she fumbled in her pocket and found them. And she coiled her hair, she rubbed off the paint and she was Auntie again, but she was a new person, too.

There was a warmth about her. She looked worn and sad, but feeling had got into her and she looked at Tom as if she cared who he was. She put her arm round him, she pulled him against her, and she cried for a bit but the milk nearly boiled over and there was bread to cut

214

— great slabs of it, and they ate cheese and ham and the last piece of Christmas cake — anything they could find, for they were famished.

6

In the outside world unrest prevailed, and communism and anarchy were spreading. In America the death sentence was passed on Sacco and Vanzetti. In Liberia secret societies of cannibals met, their teeth filed to needle-sharp points. Nearer to home, in Sydney, the Electrical Workers' Union considered a motion for the suspension from duty of the Lord Mayor because he hobnobbed with the royal party too freely. Even closer, at Port Adelaide, eighty unemployed men lived with rats in a shed on the waterfront; while, closer still (it was unbelievable) other men slept on the banks of the Torrens, and you knew them because they ran round the city carrying a wheat bag — and if the buggers didn't choose the river to bed down by, they slept in lavatories, ditches, cemeteries and drain pipes.

It was horrid, you didn't want to think of it . . . and in the Queen City, too. For it was a wonderful time to be alive in. People left their ordinary avocations for one more glimpse of the Duchess and her beautiful nature was expressed by simple words and the smile of a sunny soul. And Dame Nellie was going to sing the National Anthem in Canberra; and in Adelaide returned servicemen sang in the Town Hall, though the third verse of "Mademoiselle from Armentieres" had to be censored. And schoolchildren did mass formations on the Oval while the band played "Barcelona". And the Duke's voice was soft and pleasing, with just a faint trace of a Cambridge accent; and the Duchess had a rose-leaf complexion, she looked particularly charming and: "Oh, you wonderful one; you beauty," roared men in their enthusiasm, but some people pushed and it was disgraceful, though it had been glorious weather for the Garden Party and tonight was the Ball. And you'd be a striking figure, faultlessly dressed; you'd be in lemon-toned *satin de soie*; you'd wear a modish toilette, a handsome toilette, an effective toilette; you'd choose a becoming shade of electric blue . . .

Girlie had chosen flame *crêpe de Chine* with velvet poppies round the hem.

And that morning Boy O'Brien was a hero. He had made up his mind and it was a coloured world again. The sun blazed and he knew what to do. He opened her door and the room was dark; Boy couldn't see Jim, but he stayed brave. It had taken all night to make up his mind: now it was morning, and he'd entered her room. He went to the window and pulled up the blind. The end was beginning, and now the walls of Pearl's room were white. She stirred in the bed, she sat up. She pushed the hair-net out of her eyes and her black nightie gaped. She showed him her skinny chest and for a moment he was back in the storeroom with her snail mouth pursed to get him. But he blinked, it was easy — Boy blinked that Pearl away. This Pearl was years older and there were two Jims on the mantelpiece. Her rat mouth, her snake body meant nothing.

She was a small woman, pale, with shadows round her eyes. Her skin was greyish, unhealthy, her china-blue eyes were faded and this was Pearl now: a pale woman with wrinkles and a twitchy mouth. But she was clever, she knew tricks, she turned herself into a slum child lisping for Jesus. There was a land of pure delight where saints immortal reigned, but the child sat shivering, beseeching — surely he wouldn't turn her out? But Boy was a stony statue, Pearl couldn't get him that way, so she snarled and bared her teeth. The room went hot and muffled. Smoke writhed from black candles, there was a sweet smell of incense. A spirit form rose, like the white escaped from the cracked egg, bumping, in its pan of boiling water. There was an animal panting close and Boy was a wax doll, his tongue was a lizard in his mouth. She stuck in thorns and he'd be melted in the fire of her hate. For a while it started to happen, but then Boy hated, too — his hate was worse than Pearl's.

He hated; he grew stronger, he escaped her. He watched her face crumple and slowly she moved from the bed. Her skin was pale, clammy, like the soft underside of the soap slab; she had moles, he saw them as she dressed. She was a sleepwalker putting on clothes; she showed him her body without caring, all her power was gone. He told her she must leave. "Get out," his voice said and she was defeated, she looked wizened as she flung things in a suitcase. He told her Brother Wells was dead and a Boy Scout, too (and it could have been Tom Mundy; it might have happened to a child like the one Boy O'Brien had been).

Girlie came into the room. Pearl ran to her; she was the servant girl who pleaded in a sacking apron. She was hideous as she begged and entreated. She was ugly, quite powerless, and she'd been a woman Girlie had feared.

How could she have felt it — the fear that was mixed with love? It was all gone now. The frightened rabbit scuttled and Girlie wanted to laugh. It was pathetic, disgusting — this quivering naked thing before her. But there was Boy to look at: his suit was well cut, his profile was thrilling, and she wanted to press against him, he was the hero she'd sought all her life. He was just like Papa. She'd heard his voice shouting and it was a time before the war, it was years ago and Papa was someone steely and cruel. Girlie sighed with love as she climbed on his villain's knee. She felt his arms close about her and she sighed with the pain. It was perfect, so pleasant, and she felt little and cringing. A dizzy feeling came and she'd felt it with Pearl. Together they'd been perfectly evil, invincible, and of course it was only pretending; of course magic didn't exist. But she'd loved Pearl — she'd hated her, feared her — and together they'd seemed like one. Girlie had felt blissful, so big. She had to have someone — she must have an iron arm about her; she must belong to a person wicked and real. Boy was the only one, now. He'd been transformed, unaccountably, in a trice — and he was a soldier, he'd tramped in the mud on dead men's faces. Girlie felt dizzy. He was strong, a hero. Pearl was buttoning her coat — it was awful, last season's, with a monkey-fur collar. Boy counted out money. He thrust notes into Pearl's hand and she was gone. She left Jim behind on the mantel on either side of the remember-me pansies.

And in Adelaide on Anzac Day soldiers marched through the streets. Medals jingled sweetly as rain fell, and they came closer to the Cross of Sacrifice. Girlie stood on tip-toe, but she was always disappointed — they were always ordinary men out in the rain; she never saw anyone savage enough for a hero . . . But suddenly there was one in the house. Pearl had departed and they'd get a keeper for the old gibbering man and it would be a new life for Girlie and Boy.

He let her talk. Her voice didn't change a thing. The morning passed away; the afternoon went quicker. For a while he looked at Jim's photo, he wrote a letter telling about Swells, then it was time to dress for the Lord Mayor's Ball.

It was autumn, early evening, but the soft golden sunlight of a summer's morning seemed to have been enmeshed in the Exhibition Building. The lights were on, though it was too early for the Ball to begin. No one had come and the ballroom was empty. Its decorative scheme was charming and suggested a trim English garden with terraces and parterres, hollyhocks, gilly flowers and snapdragons.

There was no stage, for in its place stood old stone walls and tufted lawns and a fountain throwing up a cloud of crystal water. The poplars on the drop-scene at the back further added to the illusion, and one could almost hear the murmur of bees.

Overhead, ropes of asparagus fern and ivy were garlanded from the huge central light. The iron pillars supporting the balconies had been painted to resemble tree trunks (some boughs and greenery being added to aid in the delightful effect).

Pink malmaison roses and carnations decorated the tables in the supper room. Autumn tints were a feature in the smoking and card rooms.

Boy's world blazed. It was sunset and colour was every-where, his mind was suffused. In the florist's shop there'd been great pails. Shaggy marigolds stuck their heads out of dippers and they were so orange Boy wanted a bite. Once he bit, it was like eating a bird. Orange petals flew everywhere and he swallowed, it was like eating the sun. But in the pails were the tall ones: Canterbury bells, that made mauve cups and saucers; forests of carnations and larkspurs. But it was always violets the ladies bought; the criterion of feminine beauty was to have a large posy of violets tucked amidst the sables. And another good smeller was clematis, like stars, and the lilies went in moist boxes of moss. Some were shell-pink, others exquisite green, and it was green and red in the glass basket when Pearl did geraniums for the window, and once there was a midget orange tree gleaming with fruit (Papa had a great love for small trees indoors). And Boy didn't hate him any more and it was sad, but not sad at all. Papa was a florist, there was a shop with marigolds and lilies. And there was the Bristol glass basket and the bird vase, the one like a lady's slipper, and Pearl tried to get Boy in the storeroom, but now he didn't care. All his hate was burned away. It was sunset and Boy and Girlie sped through the Hills and would he do it? — he thought so, for the sunset colours were soaking everywhere; they

221

were keeping him brave. They fell on Girlie's face, they came through the trees. And Boy had loved Jim, such a good love it was, and seed packets rattled — it was mazed in his mind: everything, everyone. Jim and Pearl and Papa and Gran telling the Irish stories and the terrible saints. And Socrates had his head encircled with roses, Caesar concealed his baldness with laurels. They were things you remembered and Christmas was hot, but the shop window went white and silvery. There were little girls with ermine tippets, skating in a snowy landscape. Pearl was clever, she did it with a mirror and sprinkles of glitter. And there was holly and ropes of evergreens, robin red breasts, yule logs. Funny, really. The frost sprinkled on over artist's gum; and cotton-wool snowflakes, tinsel stars.

All these things were in Boy's mind as the Dodge sped on. It was wonderful — the sunset and his mind full of flowers and people and Christmas, and the engine accelerating and the car moving at such speed. And it was astonishing — you went over deserts, you reached the South Pole, you were carried higher than ever a bird flew into the sky: they went so rapid, and they were only bodies. Girlie had shaved legs inside her stockings and the poppies round her hem had velvet centres and she rustled so nice, her red lips were slippery, she smiled and smiled and forgot she was a body, that under her skin were blood drops; and there were bones like living pillars and the blood poured round them, it flowed, it whirled, and there'd be boars' heads for supper at the Ball and they'd had a snack before they'd started — it was to steady their tummies and the toast fingers were soldiers and all about them, now, were explosions. Boy wanted to laugh. Seed boxes were bursting and seeds tumbled out and it was autumn, quite warm, and seeds were jerking; they sprang in Jack-in-the-Box fashion, burst like pistol shots, and you'd be thrown everywhere, anywhere, and Boy wanted to laugh worse. They'd be liberated — Jim had done it before him and you'd be a seed that flew through the air, just a gust of wind would do it, and the bend was coming where confetti dots danced. Over the windscreen they shimmered, these bits of sun. Boy came so fast. And he aimed the car at the sun. They tore up, it was as if a gust of wind got them, Girlie was screaming. Up up they went at the sun and the wind blew and they sank with a beautiful twisting; they were carried so far — down, down — beyond even the trees' shadow. It was a peculiar twisting flight into a deep gorge, a deep lovely valley. Boy had driven them at the sun, off the road. Down, down they sank. There was an explosion, they were scattered far and wide.

And it was night, now, and raining which made it perfect. For the slippery pavements swam with lights and they were in strings above your head and you were roofed with flags, too, and now here they were at your feet. And by the river the unemployed shivered and hugged their wheat bags. Lights were everywhere and Victoria Square was a wilderness of Christmas trees and Holden's Band played at the Town Hall and the pie carts were hidden away. And cars crawled and ladies got out. You saw crystal embroidery, ostrich feathers, *satin de soie*, taffeta, sequins and there was red carpet going up and people cheered and there was a garden inside and you'd faint, for you saw her, a Duchess, she was charming in a diamond tiara and pearls. It didn't matter about the men by the river or how natives Far North had cyanide put in their meat when considered a nuisance. None of it was true, only tonight was. They were royal, but they looked like boy and girl. The music started and they didn't want dreamy waltzes. The Duke requested "Hi Diddle Diddle".